The Nirvana Threads

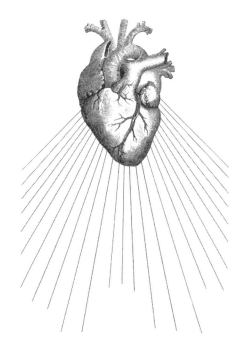

RACHEL TREMBLAY

ISBN-13: 978-0-9690172-2-6
ISBN-10: 0969017227
E-BOOK: 978-0-9690172-3-3

GrindSpark Press

For those who chase it.

Beloved of mine
Of below and above
A seed has grown
In the shade, in the sun
Towers now in my life, with blossoms and fruit
Sweetness, there is no sweeter than you
Of all the beauties
Inspiring my soul to its knees
Of all the melodies
That have bewitched me to dance
None have charmed me, none like you have
You are my divine Love
You are my eternal Romance.

Nirvana: a place or state characterised by freedom from or oblivion to pain, worry, and the external world; salvation through the union of the self with the primal source or supreme being; freedom from the differentiated, temporal, and mortal world of ordinary experience.

1 Johnny

The space between them was narrow. The smile that lived beside her just moments before had faded. His curled fingers gouged into his thighs, crumpling the fabric of his jeans. She would have reached for them. She should have. It would have been easy to hold his hand one last time. But her body was stiff, paralysed, her eyes transfixed. The moonlit trees on the horizon, the tall grasses and sign posts beyond the window behind him, all slowed to a near stop, as did her breath and the beating of her heart. Its thudding, held in time like a dripping faucet, echoed loudly in her head. She drove her chin through the mud-thick air to face the front—ahead, where there was now nothing but light.

"This is it," she thought. The boys in the front sat still, their howling quieted, their bodies no longer bouncing up and down, no longer flailing with excitement. They sat still, the chorus to Minor Threat's "Steppin' Stone" blasting from the radio, filling the car with its distortion, until it too was silenced by the screeching of metal and the shattering of glass as they collided with the oncoming semi.

"I told you this was a great spot!" Carlie flung her backpack over her shoulder and skipped towards the stopped car. Picking up hitch-hikers under a sign prohibiting hitch-hiking was ironically tempting to potential rides. Johnny was almost convinced. His back had been bent under the weight of his grumpiness since they left late that morning. But he grunted and caught up, dragging his feet because he always did. Sliding in beside her he cracked a forgiving smile.

Carlie woke up expecting that smile beside her. Instead, a dull beige flickered like an old film on reel, on and off, through the gaps of her fluttering eyelids. The room was unrecognisable. She found herself in an elevated, twin-sized bed, lying comfortably with her arms by her side. Her strange whereabouts should have bothered her, should have stopped the overpowering sense of peace from rising to the surface, but it didn't. Everything was in perfect order. She knew that, somehow, she had cheated death. She should have been thankful. Yet if she were to have died at that very moment, in the strange beige room lying in the comfortable bed, it would have been fine by her. It didn't matter. Everything was good. Life made sense. Existence, and herself in it; all of it made sense. She belonged exactly where she was.

An out-of-focus, dark-haired woman dressed in white appeared beside her; a doctor. She fiddled with Carlie's body. Muffled, incomprehensible sounds came from her mouth. Leaning in closer, she stroked Carlie's hair. The brown of her eyes was the only clearly defined feature on her blurry face. It might have passed unnoticed, but how could it, when the doctor cracked Johnny's smile, just before fading into the murkiness like a ghost.

Carlie had received a heart transplant, they told her. She had practically died on the way to the hospital. She was in horrible shape, they said. Hers was the success story they all talked about since the accident. A donor's heart had arrived too late, its intended recipient dying before he could receive it. Carlie was in such a critical state they would have never wasted a heart on her. But she was a match and the heart needed a home, quickly. Her lucky stars were aligned that day. But not Johnny's. He had died, and the other two flailing monkeys too.

The news crushed her. If there was a god, Carlie imagined him at once to be very nasty as she buckled under his punch. Unanswerable questions exploded, and from heart-wrenching incomprehension came uncontrollable screams, hurled and propelled throughout the ward and beyond. Already swamped by call-button beeps and headaches, the nurses would eventually shuffle over with drugs; sedatives that weren't meant to numb, just hush. Carlie was then free to agonise for hours on end, without sound, tears, a twitch or even a frown.

Each time she woke from under the wool sleep had pulled over her, she relived the same pain, the same screams, and the same deceptive, doped-up calm. Until at an indiscernible time, confused and tired, she came to and didn't fight. Exhaustion won. She sat back and let it come—let the heavy blow plough into her. There was a slow, underwater quality to the beating. Its momentum unstoppable, the truth finally forced its way in, sank, and settled with a deep thud.

The following days were long and morose. Carlie did her utmost to return to the harmonious state in which she had woken after the accident, remembering how strangely perfect she had felt despite her physical pain. The memory sat still in her mind, somewhat apart from the rest of the noise. Though she approached it with care, she couldn't reach it.

However, Carlie found that when she closed her eyes, colourful patterns appeared. The dark screen of her eyelids became a kaleidoscope of swirls and squares and triangles, dots and stripes. Mesmerized, she kept busy by reproducing them with the crayons and sticky pads left on her bedside table, carpeting the floor with drawings and beeping for more paper every second day. When the visuals ended, there was nothing left but to focus on rehab.

Rehab sucked. Physiotherapy was scheduled daily now that Carlie could stand, and that was at least a good way to keep her occupied. The rest of her waking hours were bumpy and dizzying, badly cushioned with the lowest quality distractions. A raggedy Danielle Steele a nurse had given her held up her head no better than an old flat pillow, and the sitcom reruns on the two available TV channels were as supportive as deteriorating couch stuffing. Carlie's friends, mostly from work, visited a few times, but quickly disclosed how little affection there was between them by not coming at all: the empty shell of a teddy bear. And her parents, a questionable bed comforter. When they heard the dreadful news, they flew two thousand miles, clear across the country from the east coast to the west, to see her perhaps for the last time. Alas, she didn't die, and they left as soon as the danger was over. Having paid the rent for her apartment while she couldn't work, her food and private room in the hospital, they assumed she had everything she needed. Their absence was nothing she wasn't used to, and although she thought she should have been saddened by it, that they weren't all of a sudden staying by her side left her indifferent. So, no comforter after all.

Hearing her brother's voice was the only buffer she had against sadness and boredom. Every day, that beige rotary phone became a dear friend, its hard, cold plastic warming her existence. It was a short moment of rest for her soul. A small, warm corner of a feather mattress.

Carlie smiled politely to her physical therapist as he rolled her off to the "get-well" gym. He helped her up.

"You know I can walk now," she said with a faint trace of humour as she reached for the parallel bars. She trudged through the motions. The pain did a good job of keeping her in the present moment, but images of the crash would creep into her head as soon as she found the slightest relief. Johnny's grasping fingers. The still, awe-struck silhouette of the bodies against the blinding headlights. And before that, Johnny's indulgent smile as he crawled into the car. His tantrum earlier that morning when he found someone had smoked the last of his weed. He just couldn't remember it was him.

Johnny. He was a kind person who saw the good in everyone, though he was the first to put himself down. A college drop-out, he hopped around from job to job, unstimulated but content. There were plenty of means to success other than through school, he would say. One had to be passionate about what one did, that was all, and sitting in a classroom had failed to evoke that magic feeling in him. So he bartended, promoted concerts, mowed lawns, cut hair. He did anything he felt like, and usually with enough nonchalance to show his lack of interest in all of that, too. The exception was Carlie. She held his interest from the first moment. From everyone else he stayed aloof, free from ties and high expectations.

As with many wounded creatures, it was just a front. He harboured profound musings, he just shared none of them. He kept them even from Carlie, though she sensed them steadily bustling behind the brown of his irises. His history was always near, a sensitive nerve just below the surface. He would often sit for hours, thinking, frowning. But he wouldn't share, and Carlie didn't push.

She knew he had been a difficult child. A trickster, an agitator, an arsonist, a thief. All before the age of twelve. Still, she had no doubt that deep down he had been a good kid, just as he had become, to Carlie, a good man. Her parents had never understood why she married him. She loved him, that was why. She loved the fiery spark in his eyes, his sense of humour, and their common love for music. And his smile. His smile that showed his good heart. That was reason enough for her.

Standing alone in the middle of the rehab gym, lost in thought, Carlie touched her lips. She remembered kissing Johnny. Her fingers trailed down her chin and flopped onto her chest. Her hand moved back and forth in a caress over her new scar, still sore, and its small, protruding staples. This heart, under her sternum, this entity that pumped her blood, she wasn't supposed to feel it, ever, they had told her. Even if she were to have a heart attack, she shouldn't feel it, because the pain was travelling someone else's nerves. It was supposed to be a numb heart. But the first few days after she woke up, when she was quiet and relaxed, she could feel its every beat. And every emanating pulse, she felt all the way to her lips that remembered kissing Johnny. But now there was only the painful squeeze of longing and regret. This heart that was not hers, how could it already be broken? How could it understand the burning grief that grew inside it? What did this heart know of love?

"Excuse me," she asked an aid walking by. He smiled as he stopped. "Whose heart do I have?"

"I can't help you with that, sweetie. Our donors are kept anonymous. But if you want to write the family an anonymous thank-you letter, we can pass it along. Just let us know." He gave her bicep a sympathetic squeeze and walked away. She watched him leave, weaving through the equipment, out into the open reception area, and out of sight around the corner. Anonymous, she repeated to herself.

There were strangers, out there in the world, that had lost a family member. Someone they loved. And now, instead, there was Carlie, and she could write meaningless words on a piece of paper for them. Who was it supposed to soothe? No thanks in the world could change what had happened, and somehow Carlie felt it would only make their grieving worse, rubbing salt into the wound. That's what it would have felt like for her, she thought, if some random person wrote to tell her that they had Johnny's heart. No one deserved Johnny's heart. And besides, what could she tell them? That the person who was meant to have the heart died, and so this young punk got it instead? Who was it originally meant for? A child? Someone who would eventually grow up to find the cure for cancer? Or a surgeon, perhaps, who would save countless lives; or a philanthropist who would dedicate his life to the service of others? Carlie was none of those things. What she was to do with such a gift, she didn't know. It was April 1994, and she couldn't think further than the next gym day. She couldn't think past Johnny's kiss.

By June, after one bedridden month, three months of rehab, weekly biopsies and all kinds of tests every few days, Carlie was given the okay to go. They stocked her with medication—pills she would have to take for the rest of her life—and an appointment with the doctor that would follow her progress in her new town. Or, more precisely, her old town. Carlie had decided to move back home to Mootpoint, somewhat reluctantly, leaving the shores of the west she had grown to love. It would be good to be close to family, and away from a life that only reminded her of him.

Her suitcases in the trunk, the taxi driver kept the motor running, as per Carlie's request, after pulling up to the cemetery gates.

"It's not open yet, miss," the driver said.

"That's okay. I won't be long." She got out, stringing her backpack over her shoulder. He watched her push herself up over the iron-wrought fence and shook his head.

It was an obligatory visit, and certainly the respectful and respectable thing to do, but she hated it. The eeriness of a plot of land populated with standing pieces of rock representing dead people, like pawns on a board game, except with bones and decaying flesh of varying degrees below the table; she hated it. Tombstones didn't represent people at all. Cold slabs of rock, with gushy words carved into them. Perhaps Johnny's deceased body was cold, but his living soul, if it was out there somewhere, had to be warm as blood. The stone, the flowers, his tiny lot, they were only mementos, and were in no way a means to be with him. Still, fresh blooms were placed, tears were shed, and she did exactly what she was supposed to do. Feel horrible.

A few hours later, she climbed aboard the spaceship, as she kept calling it, and flew high above and away from Johnny's game-board piece, wondering if his warm soul was enjoying a similar view.

2 Moot or Mars

Mootpoint. It hadn't changed. A small town of fifteen hundred, there were few corners unknown to Carlie. Its small, busy centre branched out like a star into nine smaller neighbourhoods, each resembling the other. Most streets were wide and lined with tall, deciduous trees, often with children dangling in the playground of their branches. If that wasn't enough green therapy on your way to wherever you were going, downtown was a big seventy-five-acre park peppered with leafy things of all kinds and garnished with a small, man-made lake. In under thirty minutes driving southbound, you would hit Pine Beach, a wide, sandy strip that hugged a large, ocean-feeding river. Westbound was a small mountain range, though big enough to enrich the skyline with its tree-topped edges. Empty fields, forest and farms separated the town from smaller and bigger ones north- and eastbound. The green felt as familiar and necessary to homecoming as did the old, enduring storefronts and the cobblestone crosswalks.

The family house hadn't changed either. A one-storey eyesore, it was a glorified white tissue box plopped on a mound of grass. Nearly redeeming it was a pink porch across the front, painted at the insistence of her pushy nine-year-old self during her one weeklong Barbie phase. Once a bright bubble-gum hue, it was now faded and dirty, peeling at every plank like curling hangnails. A smooth rectangle by the door still held its original colour, a testimony to the broken and discarded bench under which it had managed to dodge years of erosion. Past the front door was the living room and kitchen area, and directly down the hall was her room, left intact from five years before.

Carlie's parents, Derek and Denise, had no artistic flair, according to her. It showed in their decorating, or lack thereof, she said. The bare walls were off-white. Egg-shell or some shit, is what she called it as if it almost mattered. To Carlie it was all lifeless beige. Every other thing was dark green, black, brown. Nothing particularly pleasing to the senses adorned the shelves or ledges; nothing stuck out to feed the eyes with colour, or beauty. It was all just *meh*.

The Ds resumed their roles of not paying much attention to Carlie upon her return. They were off on yet another cruise the very next morning. What luck it was that Carlie's accident had happened before and not during, she heard them discussing that night. It didn't matter. They had their own lives and she understood that. Carlie had always been independent, though perhaps out of necessity, and they understood this. Independent, but also stubborn, eccentric, unpredictable—this was their Carlie. And they never failed to include *smart*, which was why they never understood how she could do what she did: things always a tad unhinged.

Jumping off bridges into water, or nets, or anything that would reduce the chance of death; shaving Critter and Boobs, the family dogs (RIP), in matching mohawks; sleeping out on the highest rooftops she could find for the first-class sunrises, or simply for the first-class privacy, with or without a boy; and, just perhaps, stealing the neighbourhood garden gnomes from gaudy front lawns and ceremoniously burning them in a kerosene-drenched funeral pyre as a protest to bad taste and bourgeoisie.

This was the gist of her teen years. And that was just on Mondays. Always inspired by new ways to cause a ruckus, she never had enough time to do it all. With Johnny, she had met her match. Marrying at a young age was far from the craziest thing she'd done, yet one of the hardest for her parents to stomach.

From where they sat, Carlie would be forever wild. There was no expectation that things would change now that she was back, just as they didn't expect their help or advice to suddenly be needed, or heeded. The space, although not completely cold, was wide between them. Still, it was good to be home.

"She's back!" Leo said, looking up from behind the propped hood of the red Chevy, the whiteness of his teeth brought out by his oil-marked face. He had a manly smile. Not quite as gentle as Johnny's, thought Carlie, but a million times warmer. Coming home to Leo was what coming home was really about. He rolled out from behind the vehicle, pushing the chromed handrims of his wheelchair with long, smooth thrusts. She met him halfway with a child's eagerness, falling onto his lap and into his arms at the same time.

"I missed you," she said, her face buried in his neck. "Thanks for the calls."

"You're welcome." He held her tightly, and then pushed her back a little to better look at her. "Your hair is long."

"So is yours." She stretched out a strand to his shoulder.

"And whoa, killer tatty!" He examined the black-inked whale that stretched across her inner forearm.

"Hey, Carlie!" a fellow worker called from the back of the garage. Carlie turned to see Damien, a friend of the family. His father, Fern Moore—*Pa-Fern* for the familiar—owned the shop and had hired Leo straight out of high school. Fern had taught him the ropes, and he and Damien had grown and worked side by side for the last twelve years. When Fern passed, they took on the shop together.

Carlie rose to greet him.

"Hey," Damien said again, sounding surprised as he looked at her from top to bottom, not discreetly enough for Carlie not to notice. "Your brother didn't tell me you were arriving today. It's great to see you. What the hell, Wheelo? If I'd known, I would have cleaned up a bit." He flattened out the front of his dirty blue coveralls, lifting his chin as if to appear sophisticated.

"Classy." Carlie grinned. "I'd give you a hug, but . . ." She shrugged, acknowledging his grimy outfit.

"Understandable." He nodded. "So, you're back! And in one piece. Whew. You're real lucky, you know that."

Carlie's smile vanished. "Ya."

"I mean, look at your brother. You'd think that you'd *think* before climbing into a car with random idiots."

"Ya, I get it, Damien. I didn't think. I messed up . . . again." She gave Leo a pained look. Her demeanour softened. "See you at nine?"

"You got it."

She threw a quick glance in Damien's direction and sketched a smile as she turned to leave. She didn't want to be on bad terms with her brother's oldest friend ever, and on her first day back at that.

"Uh, see you later!" he said.

They watched her leave before going back to work.

"Jackass," Leo said, tossing a dirty rag at him.

"What? She's like family to me too. She almost died, man."

Leo had also been in a car accident. He was seventeen at the time. A drunk driver had run the red light and smashed into him, crushing his legs beyond repair. He got by pretty well in his wheelchair, though, and his spirits . . . Well, they had always been unusually serene. He was the only person Carlie had missed over the last five years, and the only real joy to her return.

Carlie waited for him on the faded pink porch of her parents' bungalow, her face to the setting sun. Her mind drifted into the brushed streaks of purples and oranges, into the morning before her crash.

"I really don't think wearing a monkey suit to skydive would be newspaper worthy," Johnny said as he rummaged through his drawers.

"Yes, but . . . imagine if the parachute was also a big monkey," Carlie suggested, her eyes wandering across the ceiling as she visualised it. Johnny crouched and walked across the room on his knuckles to where she lay on the futon mattress. She giggled her way under the blankets to hide, but the ape found her, entangled in sheets and sunlight, where he held her captive in his embrace.

An Impala slowed to a stop.

"Hey, sis!" Leo called from the driver's seat, the window rolled down.

Only half out of her daydream, Carlie looked at him, her hand clutched over her heart. After a few blinks he came into focus, but she remained frozen in place.

"Are you okay?" he called to her.

After some thought she answered, "Ya, of course," and gave in to the solace of her brother's presence. She ran down the front lawn and around to the passenger side, pausing before climbing in.

"Still weird?" he asked.

"Ya, a bit."

"It'll take a while."

Leo drove them to the Mars Bar, a local pub on the edge of town, where he was a regular thanks to the easy wheelchair access, the friendly staff and the wicked music, he said. The glass door was plastered with small concert flyers and band stickers, with only a few cracks between through which to see inside. Carlie tried to peek through these as she leaned over Leo to open the door for him. With a raised finger he interrupted her and pulled out a small metal rod with plastic, curved antennas.

"Damien made this for me years back." He proceeded to twist the rod, extending it an arm's length. He squeezed the trigger on the handle. "It's my grabber! See those pliers at the end?"

Leo closed the pliers on the pub's door handle and swung it open with a tug.

The lights were bright for a club, the air hazy from cigarette smoke and warm from all the bodies. The music was loud and the chatter even louder.

"Hey Leo," said the door girl with the green hair, beaming a smile. She looked like a forest pixie with tattoos. He smiled back and handed her a ten-dollar bill, pointing to himself and Carlie.

"My sister," he said. The pixie smiled at Carlie, nodding. She then held out her hand, and in it Leo placed his. They stared into each others' eyes, just long enough for it to be uncomfortable for Carlie. Slightly taken aback—not by the fact that her brother might be in love but just by the emotion being so near—she waited, but the kiss didn't come. The door girl stamped a small, black hot-air balloon on the back of Leo's hand and he rolled away, seemingly content with that. Friendly staff is right, Carlie thought. She exposed her inner wrist, which was stamped with a tad less affection. Which was good because that would have been weird.

"Leo!" Damien yelled as he climbed over some sprawled legs to reach him. "Hey." He gave Carlie a light tap on the arm. "You're not angry with me I hope."

"I'm over it." She smiled, shrugging off his brotherly concern. A crackle popped behind them. A lanky guy with a guitar hanging around his neck was fiddling with an amp. He stepped over the carpet of guitar cables up to the mike stand.

"Hey, guys, thanks for coming out." He turned to sweep some cables away with his feet. A few whistles replied from the back corners. A short, bearded guy wearing a black trucker hat joined him on stage and threaded on the bass. Two girls in plaid school-girl skirts, ripped fishnets and army boots followed, picking up trumpets, and a guy with dreads that fell down to his thighs sat behind the drums. In the background hung a black, stretched-out curtain, with "THE JINX" spelled out in large strips of white electrical tape. The dance floor, a grid of dirty linoleum tiles, filled with people. Leo led the way further back into the club where he rolled up a ramp to a low mezzanine and up to a half-circle table pushed up flush behind a flimsy railing made of black-painted two-by-fours.

"I hope you like to boogie, 'cause we won't stop until we rock your socks off! Let's go!" the singer hollered into the mike. After four rapid drumstick counts, ska-punk blared.

"You want a beer?" Damien shouted to Carlie, sitting between her and Leo. She shrugged, smiling as she took the presented bottle. He handed one to Leo. "So how are you enjoying being back home?" he yelled.

"Um, it's only been a day, but it feels exactly the same." She strained to speak loudly enough.

"Only you're legal now," he added with a smile that was both innocent and mischievous.

She nodded, letting a grin creep through as she took a swig of her beer.

"I'm really happy to see *him*." She pointed to Leo with her bottle. He was busy watching the girls rock out to a choreographed step with their trumpets.

"He's happy to see you," Damien said. He pulled his chair a bit closer to her, leaning in to avoid shouting. "He couldn't stop talking about you over the last few months. You know, I'm really happy to see you, too. You don't seem to want to talk about it, but I gotta say, we were really scared."

Carlie nodded politely and looked at the band. She let the nod turn into a head bop. The singer was kicking his legs to the rhythm, the rest of the band pointing their instruments to the right and to the left, up and down, in synch. The drummer thrashed his head, his long dreads flying all over the place like octopus arms. The packed crowd jumped up and down and smashed into each other, while others made themselves room for moves that appeared a little more like dancing. It looked like fun. Carlie glanced over at Leo, who met her gaze, and they smiled at each other.

Leo had always been great to her. When their parents took off, which they often did, he had been the one to care for her; taking her to school and making sure she ate. Thanks to him she had always felt safe and loved. Every night he invited her to listen to his cassettes in his bedroom where they sprawled on the carpet and read sci-fi comics, sketching out their own creatures in hard-covered notebooks. These evenings became more sporadic after he met Angie, or "Poptart" to Carlie. A high-pitched, loud-laughing flake that had nothing in common with either of them. Carlie didn't know what Leo saw in her, other than her good looks. That was not a good enough reason to abandon your little sister. His girlfriend was supposed to be cool, like him. A music lover, a good listener, a poet, perhaps, with superpowers. Instead, Poptart was super*ficial,* and so self-absorbed she ended up breaking Leo's heart while he was strung-up in the hospital with broken legs. The evenings he shared with Carlie were never quite the same afterwards.

About a dozen songs in, the lights dimmed, and the music mellowed into something smoother, almost sensual, the crowd mirroring the feeling in deliberate and snaky movements. Threadlike glow-sticks of all colours were lit and moved around like squiggly incandescent wires. Carlie grinned, enchanted by the play of lights. As she narrowed in on them, she saw that the glow-sticks were branching directly from the dancers' bodies.

"Holy crow, Leo, that's amazing! What is that?"

Leo looked at her with his usual coolness, shaking his head as if he hadn't understood. She turned to Damien, who smiled at her, reciprocating her enthusiasm but without seeming particularly impressed with the slow dancing below. She looked around. The bartenders were serving clients in a regular fashion, people walked to and from the bathrooms occupied with their regular needs, and others sat and drank, watching the band. Just business as usual. And there, before them, for all to see if they just cared to look, were sleek, writhing dancers with luminous spaghetti worms slinking out of their torsos.

"What the hell?" She pushed her head further out, squinting at the show only a few dozen feet away. A skinny, dark-haired guy reached out for a chubby blond in a short red dress, and they danced face to face, hands clamped together, their foreheads touching. The threads of light that came from both their bodies sought each other out and joined in the space between them, intertwining like fingers.

"Oh!" Carlie looked back at Leo and Damien, who looked at each other and shrugged.

Damien leaned into her ear. "You wanna go down there and dance?" His breath tickled her.

"No!" she yelled, and, taming her excitement, "No, no. I'm fine right here." She folded her arms over the cheap railing and watched carefully until the song ended, a slight pinch in her anonymous heart.

"All right, thanks, you sexy people," the singer breathed into the microphone. "You're the best. See you next time."

The lights came up and the band began to take down their gear. The smiling, sweaty crowd dispersed, and some low-volume Hendrix lightly draped the laughter and clatter.

"Am I missing something?" Carlie asked Leo. "Is this normal here in Moot, and it just hasn't spread to the rest of the world yet?"

"What, slow-ska?"

"No, the lights! The lights, man . . . their chests . . . the stuff coming out of their chests." She spoke in a slightly intoxicated stutter, moving her hands around in front of her.

He raised a brow. "What did you put in her drink, Damien?"

They chuckled.

"You didn't see the lights," she said, a bit disconcerted.

Leo shook his head.

Carlie stared at him hard, trying to decipher whether he was playing her. "Fine, whatever."

The ride home was filled with chatter from the men, Leo speaking loudly over his shoulder to Damien in the backseat. Every so often Damien's eyes rested on Carlie, who stared out into the darkness through the passenger-side window.

She stumbled her way to the room she grew up in, hitting her bed hard. It was cosy, a million times better than a hospital. She dreamt of Johnny.

3 Marigolds

The morning light shone on her sweaty skin. Carlie sat up with
half her head of black hair in a big mess. She rubbed her eyes with
her fists and mindlessly made her way to the kitchen. Bottles of
pills sat between the sink and the wall. She grabbed them one at a
time, opening them and popping tablets from each with a glass of
water. After placing the glass upside down on a drying mat, she
reached for the remote from the breakfast counter and flicked on
the TV as she prepared herself some coffee. News flash. There had
been a fire in a convenience store in the next city over, possibly
arson; a corner-store robbery in one of Moot's more sketchy
neighbourhoods; and the death of the town's oldest couple, a
ninety-nine-year-old woman and a hundred-and-two-year-old
man, leaving the world a few days apart. All that excitement
within an hour's drive, told and over with in the time it took to
grind some beans.

Carlie put the coffee grounds in the drip filter and the kettle
on the stove. The weather forecast. Some rain. Some strong winds
coming later in the week.

She poured the hot water into the paper-lined cone that sat on her cup that read "Shhh . . . There's wine in here." She put her face in the fragrant steam. Footage of a lottery winner.

"Eeeee!! Oh, I cain't believe it! Oh my gawd! Woohoo!"

On the screen, a lady with backcombed, yellowy bleached hair and a blue-and-orange, flower-patterned shirt was losing her shit. She had just won three million dollars spinning a big, stupid wheel. The plastic arrow had fallen on the pineapple, and that meant she'd won.

"Oh my gawd," she said again, placing her hand on her heart. "I feel lightheaded." And she fell backwards into the arms of the person standing behind her.

"Looks like we have another fainter!" said the announcer with the bad tan and exaggerated charisma.

Just then the door opened.

"Knock, knock," the voice said before Carlie could see the face. It was Damien. Carlie gave a wordless "hi" with a nod of her chin and drank from her coffee cup.

"Just checking up on you," he said. "A little early for that, isn't it?"

"What, the news?"

He pointed to her cup.

"Oh. It's coffee," she assured him.

"Ya, those parents of yours sure like their juice. Where are they off to now?"

"Bahamas, and who knows where."

"Yeah, good for them. I wouldn't mind a cruise."

Carlie pursed her lips. Cruises weren't something she thought of with affection.

"Dude, how come you're not at work?"

"Um, Leo's holding the fort. I wanted to come here first to ask you something."

"Okay."

"Can we sit down?"

Carlie sighed, slightly annoyed. She didn't mind Damien. He was a nice guy and a good friend, but it was a little early for serious conversation beyond the one she was having with the newscaster.

"Should I take a Tylenol first?" she asked.

"No, no." He chuckled. "I hope not."

She sat on the couch facing the TV, an elbow on the couch's arm to bring her cup of coffee to her lips with less effort. He sat next to her and took her free hand, making her jerk in surprise, the coffee riding up the side of her cup and falling back down just before taking the dive overboard. She scowled at him, partly because of the close call, but mostly from wondering why he was holding her hand so damn gently, not sure if she wanted to register his bizarre, unexpected morning behaviour.

She was only a few sips in. She might as well still be dreaming.

To be safe, she put the cup down and turned to him, staring at his downcast eyes as he searched for the right words. Before he could speak, filaments of light, just like those that came from the dancers the night before, crept from his chest, through the fabric of his shirt, stretching out towards her.

"Holy shit!" She shot to her feet and backed up against the wall.

"What? I'm sorry! I didn't . . . I didn't even say anything. Was it the hand? Crap."

"What the *hell* is that?" she asked, still against the wall.

"I'm sorry, I just . . . wanted to hold your hand."

"No, not that. The lights . . . coming out of your chest!"

"What? What are you talking about, Carlie?"

He looked down at his shirt. The threads of light slinked back in, slowly. He frowned, looking back up to shake his head at her as if she was just trying to get out of the situation.

"Carlie . . . Ah, never mind. I'll see you later." He stood and walked to the door. Carlie didn't stop him. When she heard his footsteps leaving the porch she ran out and watched him drive away in his blue Pontiac.

On the screen a baby tiger was being born in a zoo and everyone was very happy about it.

Carlie showered, brushed her teeth, got dressed and let her wet hair hang loose to dry on its own. All the while, thoughts about the wiry threads of light nagged at her. Neither her brother nor Damien had seemed to notice them, and everyone else at the Mars Bar had just gone along with their business as if nothing spectacular was happening. Did no one see them? Or was this completely normal, and they were just jaded?

And now she had hurt Damien. She didn't want to cause anyone pain. An uncomfortable, yearning cramp grew in her heart. Her backpack flung over her shoulder, she stopped at the door and took a deep breath, closing her eyes before facing the world. Lighting the darkness of her mind, Johnny's image appeared before her, backlit with blazing morning light. He lifted her chin with his forefinger and tried to cheer her up with a smile. Then his gaze fell to his bare chest where a bunch of threads were wriggling out. He followed them with his eyes as they floated toward Carlie, reaching for the same lights that were coming out of her.

"Damn!" She dropped her bag to the ground and pinched the bridge of her nose, keeping her eyes closed in fear she'd see the lights she thought might really be there. She peeked. They weren't. Backpack re-slung, she headed out the door, carrying her uneasy emotions with her.

The sun was out. The air was light, infused with a cheery mood that contrasted with Carlie's. Faces were lit up with smiles and wannabe smiles lurking beneath taut skin just waiting for the opportunity to crease with joy. A white-haired lady walked her little white-haired dog on the opposite side of the street. They shared the same round, frizzy haircut. Twins. She waved at Carlie, who waved back with only a little reticence. Her feet hit the sidewalk as a cyclist flew by a few steps away, the chime of his bell trailing behind him. She felt as though she had just woken from hibernation and emerged in a different world. It was the first beautiful day of summer, so in a way it was a new day, and everyone felt it.

Carlie walked to Java the Hut, a longstanding coffee shop in the centre of town, to grab another "mug of wine" and took it with her to the park a few streets away. A picnic table sat at the edge of the lake, overshadowed by a large tree. She sat atop it, pulled out a notebook and began to sketch the shape of a woman in a tight suit, cape in the wind. Birds flew overhead, making their presence known to her by their song. One made her look up by landing in the grass before her. Digging into her bag, she pulled out a granola bar and flicked a piece at it.

"Deluxe dining today," she said.

"That can't be good for his figure," said someone approaching her from the side. A tall guy in a red hoodie smiled as he leaned over and handed her an eraser. "You dropped this." He waved his hand without raising his arm and kept going.

Carlie, struck by the young man's ease at weaving in and out of her bubble without quite popping it, impulsively decided to pop it herself.

"Hey, wait," she called out. He turned around but stayed where he was, squinting from the sun that hit him in the eyes, his face forced into a smirk. Carlie realised she had nothing to say.

"Um, it's a revolt against the imposed avian norm," she said, pointing to the weight-gaining bird. He nodded, his smirk now a grin, and walked back.

"May I?" He took a seat atop the table beside Carlie as she scooched over. They looked at the lake for a few moments.

"Self-portrait?" he asked, referring to her drawing.

"Oh, ya, I wish. Check out her pipes."

The superhero flaunted nicely sculpted biceps.

"Super-heroine," he suggested.

"Shero."

"Of course. So, you new to town?"

"Actually, I'm from here. Just came back. I was on the west coast for the last five years." Her eyes dropped as the uninvited memories of the crash invaded her head, jeopardising the easiness of the moment. "Moot hasn't changed a bit since I left. Well, hardly."

She thought about the weird, skinny light worms.

"You okay?"

Carlie raised her head. "Huh?"

"You've been silent for a good"—he looked at his watch —"three minutes."

"Oh shit, I'm sorry. Just . . . thinking about some weird stuff I saw. Huh. Sorry."

"Lucas." He smiled, his hand extended.

"Carlie. Nice to meet you."

They shook hands and chuckled.

They spent the afternoon on that tabletop. At one point Lucas ran off to get sub sandwiches, and they picnicked in the small space between them, chatting about heritage architecture, animal rights, and aliens. Carlie mentioned the accident and tried to downplay it, more to avoid pity than to deny her guilty feelings for hanging out with a boy so soon. In any case, they were just talking. There was no harm in it. That's what she told herself, trying to ignore the soft blond curls that landed on his tanned skin and fell into his bright, blue eyes. There was a soothing sweetness to feeling charmed, and that was harder to ignore.

"You got a heart transplant? Wow, that's huge. And here you are, drawing *sheroes* and fattening up birds in a Mootpoint city park."

"Ya, it's hard to believe," she muttered.

"What happened to the other passengers?"

"They all died." She looked him straight in the eyes, giving in to the memory. "My . . . boyfriend, Johnny, he was sitting beside me."

The uplifted energy of the afternoon waned into that gaze. Lucas understood that this girl was carrying a lot of baggage, but also an incredible fire. His eyes traced the contours of her face, noticing the dark freckles lining the tops of her cheeks, and her clear, brown eyes that stared at him from under long, dark lashes. The sound of ducks landing in the water helped her look away. For the next while they were silent, watching, listening, and breathing in the new summer's earthy smell.

"Walk with me?" she asked. They gathered their things.

The shops in the downtown streets were almost all the same as before, with only a few changes and additions. It all felt very familiar to Carlie yet so different. Like a worn-out pair of shoes that have been stashed in the closet for years, and when finally put back on feel funny because you just don't wear glittery flats anymore. She was not the same person as when she left. She had grown in all sorts of ways, revelled in a panoply of good times, and suffered at the hand of bad luck and self-inflicted misery— despite her best intentions—that dulled the shine of any childhood glitter. It had been five years of fireworks, both beautiful and painful.

They arrived in front of Fern's garage.

"My brother works here," she said.

Lucas looked over the battered, wooden sign that read "The Vintage Shop" in cursive, red, peeling paint.

"Nice."

Carlie went ahead through the always-rolled-up, wide garage door. It was dark inside, compared to the summer sun. Leo rolled out of the shade just as Lucas joined Carlie by her side.

"Hey, sis," he said, some concern in his tone as he eyed the stranger. "Who's this?"

"This is Lucas. We just met, in the park."

"Hey." Lucas reached out his hand.

"Leo," he replied, accepting the shake.

"He'll be studying engineering at MPU this fall. He just got here a week ago." Carlie's voice trailed off as she noticed Damien approaching. His innocent, round eyes narrowed at the sight of Lucas and hopped back to Carlie. He stayed some steps back, clearly bruised.

She pulled up an awkward smile, looked at the men one after the other, and dropped it.

"Look, uh, we're going to see Pawns & Marigolds tonight. They're playing at the Skits. Do you guys wanna come?"

"Ah, I'll be working late on this Triumph. I promised a client it'd be ready by tomorrow," Leo said.

Carlie looked up at Damien.

"Ya, no thanks." He pinched a smile and retreated to the depths of the garage where his form was engulfed in cars, racks and lifts.

Carlie looked at Leo, who curled his lips and raised his eyebrows, suggesting that he knew about Damien's failed attempt at speaking with her.

"Such is life." He rolled around to go back in and added over his shoulder, "Enjoy yourselves!"

The Skits had a classic theatre feel, with its decorated ceiling and ornate railings. There were tables and chairs on the mezzanine and balcony, but Carlie and Lucas were on the cleared parterre near the stage, checking out the gear as they waited for the band to come on. The emptiness that came with their early arrival was quickly replaced by hundreds of bodies who all huddled as close as possible to the coveted front and centre, which Carlie and Lucas had secured for themselves before the flood rushed in.

Though it was emo punk, Carlie danced slowly, at first, so her heart would know to accelerate; this numb heart of hers didn't have the necessary nerves through which to be told to beat faster. Her fight or flight reflex was gone forever, so she needed to start slowly, until her pulse picked up.

Squeezed between the moving warmth of others, Carlie felt the bass thump in her heart. It was a wonderful, familiar thump.

Intimate even. One she could curl up and fall asleep with. She closed her eyes and let her senses take over, her heart aching with pleasure as she danced, perhaps just a little harder than she should.

When she opened her eyes, her good feelings screeched to a stop. The hellish wires of light were back. And this time, transgressing the boundaries of privacy, they came from her. They were already a few feet out, floating, surreal, bright yellow and green. She could feel them, from under her skin, beneath her ribs, deep in her flesh, growing out from her heart, intertwined with her pulse and the thumping of the bass.

But her panicked breathing subsided as she realised: they weren't hellish at all. They were good. Strange, but good. So, she relaxed, and began to dance again, watching as they snaked further out. Delicious sensations spread through her body—through her arms, her torso, the base of her skull, the back of her legs, the soles of her feet—making her tingle with anticipation. Shivers ran up and down her skin. With an acute awareness crystallising, she danced a bit harder, and harder, letting her feelings build up, the heat of the room rise, the volume crescendo as the song approached its melodic climax, and when it did, threw herself into to the ecstasy that had by then invaded her completely. Her grief, always in the background, sombre and heavy, lifted like floating ashes, leaving her feeling lighter than she had in months. In years, even. In all her wildness, she had never experienced the likes of this. She flung her head back and laughed.

A hand touched her wrist. It was Lucas, a smile across his face, his skin covered in pearls of sweat. He was pretty damn cute, she let herself acknowledge. She turned her body to him, her lights shrinking to fill the space between them. Carlie stared into his eyes, savouring her secret, laughing as they danced together.

Beautiful, glowing blue strings sprouted from Lucas. Eyes wide, Carlie's first reaction was fright, despite how much she was enjoying her own. The tips of their threads touched, and, replacing all fear, was a blast of euphoria, bursting through her body and soul. Her eyes shut as she travelled inward, rolling under the strength of the sensation like the breaking point of an ocean wave. She resurfaced to a smiling Lucas staring at her. Jumping back eagerly into the moment, they cut loose, their lights becoming more and more deeply entangled.

She didn't understand what this was, but she loved it.

4 Teddy Bears and Picnics

There were serious cracks running through the peach-coloured paint of Carlie's bedroom ceiling. Broken spiderwebs covered in clumps of dust hung from random spots, swaying dreamily. There was a hole, the size of a pinky, almost directly above her head. Carlie wondered what kind of critter could fit through that hole and if it might crawl onto her at night, perhaps into her ears, or mouth, as some say spiders do, for her to then swallow. She lay in bed, thinking about laundry and other unimportant things, feeling her breath rise and fall. Yesterday's memory lurked close. She wanted to savour it, so she let it drip through between other mundane thoughts, slowly, like saline, and licked the imaginary sweetness from her lips.

"Paradise," she mouthed to herself.

She rolled onto her side. Her eyes jumped from object to object, old things that she had long grown out of but never had the heart to throw out. Sitting against her mirror was a porcelain doll in a polka-dot dress her dad had given her for no particular reason when she was about seven; on a shelf mounted to the wall opposite the foot of her bed was a sculpture of a sitting greyhound she had carved out of clay in grade nine; and below it on the work desk facing the window, covered in dust, a wooden game of chess. She hadn't grown out of that per se, but she knew she would never play again. Her mind wandered.

The sunroom. They loved to hang out there, especially in winter since it was the warmest place in the apartment. It was a narrow space, but there was enough room for a couch and a small coffee table, and walled with windows it felt much larger than it was.

"Haaa, check maaate!" Johnny sang proudly. He always won, so Carlie didn't understand what the big deal was.

"I hate this game," she said.

"You looove it! And I love you." He pulled her chin closer with his finger. She lunged into his arms.

Carlie put her hand on her chest, over her anonymous heart. Whatever it was she had shared with Lucas the night before, it wasn't love. Of course not; she hardly knew him. It couldn't compare to what she felt for Johnny. Not even close. It would be a long time before she got to that finish line again, if ever.

What was it she felt through the threads, then? Was it just the music? Warmth gushed through her as she let herself fully remember.

Carlie threw down a stack of papers in front of Leo, lifting a bum cheek onto the edge of his crowded desk.

"Today's the day," she said.

"I don't think you'll need that many," Leo said, wheeling his way out to the side to face her. "In fact, you don't need any résumés at all. You know you can work here. There's a lot we could use your help with."

Carlie looked over at Damien who was lying on a creeper under a black vintage Cutlass.

"I don't know that it would be a good idea, Leo. I need to try my luck elsewhere first. Plus, these cars are beautiful, but I don't know much about them."

"That's a minor detail." Leo saw she wasn't about to change her mind, so he dropped it. "You should probably wash that off better, then," he said, noticing the red elephant stamp on her hand. "How was the show?"

"Oh-my-god-it-was-amazing," she blurted. Realising she wouldn't be able to explain her overenthusiasm, she kicked it down a few notches. "The band was great. So good."

Leo frowned and turned his head slightly, peering at her from the corner of his eyes.

"What?" Carlie asked. "With Lucas? No, no, we're still getting to know each other, you know? It was just really good to rock out."

Satisfied, Leo rolled back to his desk where he pulled out a sheet of paper. On it was a list. "I told them you were looking and that they would be lucky to have you."

He handed it to her.

"Oh wow, thanks Leo!"

She bent down to kiss him on the cheek and jumped off the desk.

Damien pushed himself out from under the car and lifted his head to watch her go. He peered at Leo, and pulled himself back under.

"You know, if you don't tell her, you're going to be stuck just like this, watching her from a distance." Leo rolled over to him. "She's gonna date guys and live her life, and you're gonna regret having chickened out."

Damien was still under the car. He turned his head towards Leo's wheels, parked right beside his face. He didn't have anything to say to that, because he knew it was true. It wasn't the first time he had held back from telling someone how he felt, only to have them take off with someone else. He waited for Leo to roll away before going back to work.

"Let's go dancing again!" Carlie said later that day after her job hunt.

"Again?" Lucas said as they sat down on a bench outside Java the Hut's.

"Ya! It'll be fun! Didn't you just love it last night?"

"Ya, ya, it was pretty great."

He frowned at her, wondering why she showed so much zest. Yesterday she was calm and cool, with a real down-to-earth headspace, maybe even a little morose. He wasn't sure where her giddiness came from, or if he liked it.

They drank their coffee and watched the people walk by, spotting those with the ugliest hats, muttering fake conversations between them in bad, foreign accents.

"There's something else I thought we could do tonight," he said as the comedy died down. Carlie looked up, slightly disappointed, but the confidence in his smile was enough to convince her.

That evening he showed up at her doorstep with flowers. Along with the black sports jacket, it made for a pretty clean impression. White t-shirt, ripped blue jeans, black sneakers, red backpack. Freshly shaven. The package was good.

"Trying to impress me?"

He took her by the hand. Walking down her street and then along the main road through town, they hit an industrial dirt path about half an hour later.

"Yes, but they're highly over-priced," Lucas said.

"Vintage cars are like art. They're worth it. Besides, if ever you wanted one, we have the hook up." Carlie kicked some rocks as she walked.

"How come you don't have one?"

The corners of her mouth dropped and she looked ahead.

"I can ride with Leo."

"Your brother, he seems like a good guy. That other dude, though, he was looking at you pretty weird yesterday."

"Damien? Oh, he's a teddy bear."

"Teddy bear, huh? Is he your ex?"

She searched his eyes to find the jealousy she heard in his voice. "No, we never dated. He's just been around Leo and me for so long, he's like family. He's just looking out for me, you know?"

"And he doesn't like me."

"I don't know. But I do." Carlie laced her fingers through his, and then let go and started running. Lucas chased her only about a hundred feet before she began to slow down, finally stopping with her hands on her knees.

"You okay?" he asked.

She nodded, panting.

He put a hand on her back and waited for her to catch her breath.

"I just can't start so fast." She wheezed, pointing to her heart. After a few minutes, she stood straight. "I'm okay. Let's go."

They reached an abandoned factory at the end of the road. Carlie checked the door, which was bolted shut, before she noticed Lucas climbing in through a broken window, the protruding pieces of glass already cleared off the frame. She followed him through. The buzzing light post outside illuminated the first steps with a dull yellow, only hinting at unrecognisable shapes a few feet in. The rest of the room was bathed in obscurity. Carlie ran her hand along the wall, looking for a switch.

"Come," Lucas said from deeper in.

Broken glass crunched under her feet, and a smell of dampened wood stirred as they made their way blindly to the back.

"You've been here before?" Carlie asked, holding his hand as he led her through.

"Ya."

"How is that, if you've just moved here?"

"I kind of like to look for these sorts of places."

"Rotting buildings on the outskirts of town? Are you some sort of psychopath killer? Am I completely screwed?"

"Pretty much. Except for the psychopath killer part. Okay, here we go."

He began climbing tight spiral stairs, Carlie right behind, a metallic echo ringing out from their steps. The rough feel of the curling paint scratched their palms as they held the rusty railing.

"Creepy," Carlie said.

Lucas lifted a trapdoor and climbed out, reaching down to help Carlie make her way onto the roof.

"Whoa, this is awesome," she said, slightly winded, peering out at the little patch of lights that was their downtown.

His backpack zipped open, Lucas pulled out a blanket, which he spread out, a bottle of wine, which he opened, and two paper cups, which he held in one hand, the bottle in the other. He called her over with a sideways nod.

"This is nice." She accepted a paper cup from Lucas as they sat down. The rooftop, the dark, night-drenched surroundings . . . this was the kind of thing she would have done with Johnny, she realised, sighing.

"You all right?" Lucas asked.

"Ya. Just takes me back."

He wrapped an arm around her. Her broodiness gave her a mysterious charm; he liked that. They watched the lights and drank a bit without saying much, some far away crickets and toads filling the gaps with their gossip.

Sensing Carlie's body relaxing against him, Lucas put his drink down. Gently, he reached for her face, turning her head towards him. His palm on her cheek, he brushed his thumb over her eyebrow and looked into her eyes, wondering what secrets she kept in there.

"I really want to know you," he said.

He pulled himself nearer, and Carlie's heart stuttered. He was predictable, but the moment was sweet nonetheless, and she wanted to let herself be carried away in it. Her eyes half closed, she gazed at his lips, expectant. Guilt, ugly and finger-pointing, crawled out from the back of her mind where she had kept it subdued and curtained since her first encounter with Lucas. *Traitor*, it hissed as it clawed and pinched. Her frown was met with another brush of the thumb, and memories of Johnny flooded her. She closed her eyes. *Selfish*, she heard whispered within her. It wasn't Johnny's voice.

"I'm only human," she whispered back to herself out loud.

"Aren't we all." Lucas brought his face closer to hers. She felt his warm breath on her skin. She wanted to be loved again, to hold that healing, nourishing light close to her heart. Though this wasn't love. This was icing on a cake she didn't know the flavour of yet. But she wanted this moment, this tinge of delight. Easy and careless and pain-free.

"Just a kiss," she murmured. Claiming that desire, the thought of Johnny bowed out and sailed away, the whispering guilt trailing behind in his wake. Her brow became smooth, like the settling ripples of disturbed water. A sigh invited Lucas in. Her eyes closed, and his lips finally touched hers, waking a sensual thirst from another far, blanketed corner. The delectable joining of their mouths loosened her joints, and, as she sank into him, she felt the sweet threads of light sprouting from her heart. They instinctively joined with his and filled her with complete bliss.

Carlie ran up to the fluorescently lit garage, jumping over a box of tools. Damien watched her. He knew what was happening.

"Leo!" she called.

"He's out," Damien answered, walking out towards her.

"Oh." She stood awkwardly in the middle of the garage. "I didn't see you there. So stealthy."

"Sorry, I didn't mean to scare you." He stopped before he reached her. He turned and walked towards the exit instead. Carlie followed.

"So, you seem to be settling in to your new life pretty well?"

"Um, ya, I'm doing pretty good, I guess. I got a job down at the Cave?" she said, wondering if that would satisfy his curiosity. He leaned back on the hood of a big, grey car, parked with its nose at the edge of the open garage door facing the empty lot outside. He nodded at the information. She sat on the hood of the car next to him.

"And, um, my body's feeling pretty good, like . . . less pain, you know, and my chest bone doesn't hurt so much." She put her hand over it. "And I feel better up here, too. A lot better." She tapped her index to her temple, not convinced about the truth of that statement.

Damien smiled, satisfied.

"You've been going out a lot. With that guy."

"Keeping tabs, are we? Well, just a bit, really. I wanted to go dancing last night but we ended up drinking wine on the roof of an old abandoned factory down some lost road off the Main. We could see the city lights perfectly."

Damien looked away. Again, guilt crowded her.

"He's a real nice guy, you know. I understand you want to protect me, in a way, like a big brother, but really, I'm okay."

"A big brother." He looked ahead into the parking lot where the sun shone on a few gulls hustling for some old tossed fries. "Just stay true to yourself, okay? That's the Carlie I love."

The words sent a buzz through her frame. One in particular. One that shouldn't be tossed around. She observed him watching the birds squabbling over scraps, flapping and jumping on each others' backs and falling off clumsily. There was some squawking, a bit of aggressiveness perhaps. Leo rolled up amidst their silent spectating.

"Hey, you guys." He squinted, trying to read the mood.

"Ah, hey Wheelo," Damien said.

"I got a job!" Carlie announced, hopping to the ground. "I start tonight. I'll be working the bar at the Cave. You know, where people go while they wait for a table to free up in the Hillside Grill? Drinking away all their food money. It should be interesting.

I get to choose the music, so that's wicked. You should come by later."

"Right on, sis. Well, when you're done with that, you can come work here," he said as he wheeled into the shop. Carlie looked over at Damien, and their gaze locked for long enough that it should've been uncomfortable, but it wasn't. And then she saw the tips of bright, shining threads poke out from his shirt.

"Damn it."

"What?" Damien felt as if he had somehow screwed up again, although he didn't know how.

"Uh, I forgot my wallet . . . at home. I need it for . . . the paperwork, at work. You know, first day," she said with a fake sigh and smile. Then she gave him a real smile and took off.

5 The Chase

"Here's your apron, and you can stash your things back here,"
said the restaurant manager. He was a short fellow. With his long
dark hair pulled back in a low pony tail and sharp trimmed
moustache, he would have been a great model for a villain in
Carlie's sketchbook. She could even imagine his story. *Tiny villain
with pointy moustache takes over the world with bad karaoke.* She
followed him around as he explained the job, all the while musing
on his evil side and potential singing skills.

The Cave was a closed-off joint connected to the main
restaurant by a heavy glass door under an arched doorway, and
with its own extra door leading straight outside. It had limited
seating at wooden tables, with chairs that creaked and wobbled
just enough to make you feel slightly unsteady, extra supporting
pieces nailed to them in all sorts of places. On the floor, a multi-
coloured collection of cracked tiles boasted a variety of flower and
abstract patterns that played off the colourful Mexican art replicas
on the walls. The light of the floor-to-ceiling windows brought the
place to life during the daytime, camouflaging the dinginess that
became more apparent at nightfall. Among the suspended plants

was a collection of wind-chimes that hung from the big wooden trusses running the length of the ceiling, all ringing gently each time either of the doors opened. The Cave might have been run down but it was definitely cosier than its food-providing neighbour.

"You're right, Damien, she seems rather happy lately," Leo said as he shifted gears with the paddles at his steering wheel.

"And you think it's because of that *guy*? That's ridiculous. She just met him."

"Maybe. I mean, there's nothing like new love to forget an old love."

"You know it's not that simple, man. Her old love *died*. And *she* almost died. And she got a new *heart*, and left her new *home*. That shit is so heavy. I think if she's happy, for real, it comes from more than just a new dude in her life, no matter how cute he is."

"I sense jealousy," Leo said. "Look, I don't know why she's feeling so 'up'. But if it is because of the guy, just know, Carlie has some pretty high standards. She wouldn't be hanging around with him if he was a dingbat."

Damien didn't seem convinced.

"Johnny, rest in peace, he didn't seem like the most outstanding kid," Leo continued, "but I imagine he had some pretty big redeeming qualities for her to marry him."

"What did he do?"

"For work? I don't know. Nothing stable or serious, I think. But whatever he did was enough for Carlie. He was gold to her."

Damien winced. Competing with gold would be difficult.

"She never hesitated to dump her previous boyfriends the second they were jerks to her. So, I'm more worried for Lucas than I am for Carlie," Leo said with a chuckle.

"Did she have lots? Of boyfriends?" Damien asked nonchalantly, looking out the window.

"Some, ya? What's this, Damien? You got some serious hots for her, huh?"

Damien threw a dismissing glance at him. "Hots," he scoffed.

Leo smiled, looking at him and then at the road a few times over. "Really, huh? Love?"

Damien didn't answer.

Leo nodded. "Well, I feel for you, man."

"It's okay. I'm just gonna wait for Lucas to mess up," Damien said.

"Ho ho, that's rough, man. *The waiting list.*"

They parked outside the Hillside Grill. Damien hauled out the wheelchair, while Leo swung his legs out the driver's side. Being handicapped had slowed him down at first but he had been getting around perfectly for years now, doing everything he found important to do. And what he couldn't do seemed to fall to the bottom of his priority list without any bitterness.

He lifted himself into his chair with ease and rolled up to the ramp near the main doors.

"I forgot what a dump this was," Damien said, looking around as they made their way in.

Leo smirked and pointed to the ceiling. "New light fixtures."

"Really?" asked Damien, puzzled as to why Leo would have noticed what the old ones looked like.

"No, I have no idea."

The arched doorway of the Cave was in the wall on the left. The words "where waiting time is fun time" were written along the outer edge of the fake bricks lining the arch. Leo went in first.

"Hey!" Carlie sang when she saw the pair come in.

"There's some empty tables out there," said Leo to Carlie as she stepped out from behind the counter. "Why are there so many people in here?"

"They like it here." She gave Damien a friendly nod.

Damien looked around. All the customers had small, lit candles on their round bar tables, a little bowl of olives and peanuts, and a vase of flowers beside their drinks.

"I can see why," he said. "You treat them too well. They'll never leave if you keep that up." The double-entendre of his words made him grimace. It seemed impossible to him how Lucas could ever be a jerk to her, that she might dump him, seeing how sweet she was to people she didn't even need to pamper at all.

"Beer and peanuts, Carlie. That's a meal in itself," Leo said.

"Not to worry. I have a plan if they linger too long. Watch me test it?" Carlie disappeared behind the bar. There was a click and some white noise, and then highly distorted punk blasting through the speakers suspended in the corners of the little bar. The customers looked up, some annoyed, others pleased. A few, getting the message, got up, threw on their jackets and headed for the arched door, waving at Carlie on the way out.

She turned the music down a bit and came back out from behind the bar, pulling out a stool in front of Leo.

"Bah, so what if some of them stay," she said. "The owners get their money one way or the other, right? So, hey, you're here! Thanks for coming by."

"Of course. I'll be able to picture you better when you share your anecdotes. Also, I wanted to invite you and Lucas for dinner tomorrow night, at my place. With Hazel, and Damien, naturally."

"Oh." Carlie's eyebrows rose. "Okay, um, sure. I'll ask him."

She eyed Damien, surprised that he'd want to be around her and Lucas together. He didn't seem too fond of her choice. Damien answered her questioning eyes with a gentle smile.

The dinner table was lush with food. Bread puddings, chutney, baguettes, cheeses, and pickles were spread in small dishes, the large bowls filled with green salad, steaming brown rice, and lentil curry.

"Holy mackerel, Leo! It smells so good!" Carlie placed her backpack on the ground by the door as she walked in. Lucas closed the door behind them.

"Ah, it's mostly Hazel who worked her magic," Leo said as the green-haired pixie leaned over and gave him a kiss. She then came and greeted Carlie with a hug and gave Lucas a peck on both cheeks.

"I'm happy to finally meet you properly, Carlie. Make yourselves at home. We're almost ready to eat," she said with a French accent as she headed back into the kitchen.

Carlie looked into the adjacent room on the right. The TV was on. Damien sat in an armchair watching it, a beer bottle tucked between his legs. He had grease stains on his hands and his hair was scruffed. A few seconds went by before he noticed she was standing there.

"Oh, sorry! The playoffs, you know." He pulled himself away from the basketball game and walked up to the guests, greeting Carlie with a soft kiss on the cheek, something he didn't usually do. He shook Lucas' hand firmly.

"Hi, man, nice to meet you, properly. Damien."

Lucas's eyes widened, his body rattling from the vigour of the handshake.

"Uh, ya, for sure. Lucas." He wiped his hand on his pants once he got it back.

They ate and chatted, passing the bowls of food around.

"Oh man, I loved that song so bad, I played it steady for weeks! Leo begged me to stop, saying it was giving him headaches, stomach aches, even *nausea*. He couldn't take it anymore," Carlie chortled. "It was such a bad song!"

With a deep breath, Leo started singing the eighties' song of his nightmares. Lucas eyed Carlie strangely, as he had been doing all evening. She seemed so happy, so different from one moment to the next. He wasn't sure what to make of it.

This had not passed unnoticed by Damien, who sat right in front of him. There was something about Lucas he didn't trust. He could see him looking at Carlie with puzzlement, maybe even annoyance, taking no part in the conversation, eating his food way too seriously.

"What about you, Lucas?" Damien asked, cutting through the din. The others hushed.

"What's that?" Lucas asked, seeming uninterested.

"Did you ever love a song that drove everyone else up the wall?"

"Nope."

Carlie looked at Damien with big eyes. Thinking Lucas *Grumpy Pants* would be better off not seeing how badly she wanted to laugh, she held her hands to her face like visors just long enough for it to pass. Damien had never seen Carlie so giddy before, not even as a teenager. He couldn't accept that this ordinary, clearly unappreciative dude was the cause of all this joy.

Every so often, Damien's eyes would meet Carlie's from across the table, across the bowls of steaming food and reaching arms, and, in that moment, they would exchange something . . . Something that dared not be named; something warm and homey. And beautiful. And just as quickly, the moment would be swept back into the laughter and clinking of drinks.

Later that night, sitting on the couch in his studio apartment, Lucas asked her about it.

"So, what's up with Damien?"

"What do you mean?"

"You know what I mean. You were googly-eyeing him all evening."

"No, I wasn't." Carlie thought back to see if what he said was true.

"Well, clearly he wants you."

"Again with this. Don't worry, Lucas. I want *you*." Carlie threw her arms around his neck and kissed him, swinging her leg over his lap. Forgetting his jealousy, he wrapped one arm tightly around her waist and the other behind her back, leaning into her, on top of her. They wriggled down the couch to make more room for their legs, their lips and tongues moving with the waves of heat they created. His hand crawled under the hem of her shirt, slid up to her breast and squeezed, just a little too roughly.

"Ow." Carlie pulled away to look at him. Without meeting her eyes, he pushed his face into her neck.

Carlie blinked, a sudden wakefulness snapping her out of her daze.

"Wait," she said.

"Shhh." He kissed her skin, locking his body tighter with hers.

"No, Lucas . . . wait." She squirmed. "Stop."

She struggled to look down at her chest, where his hand still moved under her shirt. She looked at his chest too. Sure enough, there were no threads. No lights, no tingles, no bliss. Zero magic.

She grunted, trying to push him off. "Would you . . ."

"What is it?" He huffed, giving her a sliver of space.

"I don't know. Something's off." She looked down at her chest again.

"Oh, I'd say it's on," Lucas said, plunging back over her like an octopus.

"No, no, no." She tried to push him away again, but this time he didn't budge, trapping her. She stiffened as he became more eager. Unable to pull herself out from underneath him, a slight panic eked through.

"Lucas!"

"Just relax," he whispered into her ear as he kissed it, his groping hands reaching down to unbutton her pants.

"Lucas!" she growled.

Channelling all her strength into her arms, she shoved his shoulders off her. He sat up, irritated.

"What the hell, Lucas?"

"What?"

"What?" she repeated, thinking he had to be daft. "Damn it, Lucas. Look. We have to pause this."

"Pause?"

"Like, postpone it, maybe. I need to figure some stuff out."

Lucas brushed the invisible dust off his pants as if he were flinging her rejection away with loathing. He went to the fridge.

"You want something?"

"No, I'm going to take off."

"Really? Why? Stay here."

"No, I need to be alone."

He walked back to the edge of couch, towering over her with a beer in his gesturing hand.

"So what, you spend the whole evening happy as can be, laughing, a fucking ray of sunshine, and now that we're here alone, you're gonna just turn that off? You're gonna *lead me on*, and go home? What's the deal, Carlie?"

"There's no deal," she mumbled, taken aback by his sudden burst of anger. It was true that it did in fact turn off, though. Her lights did. On the roof, they were on. She was open, the threads magical and sweet, and now, even before she checked, before his lust made him forceful, nothing came from her heart for him. No feeling. How fickle.

"Sure there's no deal. I'm sure it has nothing to do with Damien. What a tease you are. Just leave already. Your happy fucking high is irritating anyway."

Stung, Carlie gathered her things, swallowing down the lump growing in her throat. She looked over at him through blurry eyes on her way out, the back of his head a dark shape against the light of the western he was now watching. She stepped out and closed the door to the sound of neighing and gunshots, but nothing from him.

The next days were glum. Carlie didn't call Lucas, nor did she drop in at the garage. But she went to work, and her mood could be felt there by all. The regulars who had grown to like her gave her curious glances, deciding to not overstay their welcome as they usually did.

"Take care of yourself, Carlie," said one man as he left. Carlie, resting her elbows on the bar with her chin in her hands, looked up at him and dropped her eyes just as quickly. She stared at a couple sitting in the corner. The woman reached for the man's tie sitting across from her, laughing about something. The tie was funny. Or, he looked funny in the tie. Carlie couldn't figure it out. What she did see for sure was the bliss threads they shared. They were bright blue. Pink. Yellow. Strings of light all over the place, fiddling with each other as their real fingers were.

On the way home, she saw a woman in the park playing with her young daughter. The same glowing strings travelled between them. Carlie saw them everywhere, connecting people to one another. Connections she knew felt like pure bliss. Magic. Where had hers gone?

The line-up was long, but Carlie bypassed it as if she knew what she was doing, ticket in hand. She thanked the doorman with a smile and made her way through the scattered clusters of people, and down to the bar where she ordered a drink. The music was hardly loud enough to overpower the jangle of voices and clanging bottles. And laughter. Always there seemed to be laughter. Carlie wondered how there could always be something, somewhere, to laugh about. *She* wasn't laughing. She leaned against a wall on the ground floor and sipped her drink, watching the people come and go.

"Come on, you have to find this one funny," Johnny said as he imitated yet another of their friends in farm-animal version. Finally Carlie cracked and snickered. She had been feeling blue for the past month. She and Johnny had been expecting a baby, but it didn't stick. It was more painful than she could have imagined, losing it, even if she had only known for a few weeks. It had been a long few weeks of shock, fear, and joy. And then sadness. Johnny felt Carlie slipping away from him, just out of reach, and he worked hard to keep her heart in the game. He dragged her around town on free museum days, he took her out for ice cream, he goofed around, a lot, and he took her to concerts. They loved going to shows.

Amidst the scattered bodies, Carlie saw Johnny come up close to her, taking her hands in his. He locked his big brown eyes on hers.

"Stop chasing it, Carlie," he said.

Her drink shook in her hand as someone bumped into her on their way into the crowd. The band had just come on and the floor was packed with people; and Johnny, obviously, was gone. Carlie put her drink down and squeezed into the centre of the floor.

It was Blinded Mice, hardcore melodic punk, one of her and Johnny's favourite bands. She wouldn't have missed it for the world, even if only accompanied by her memories.

The first guitar chord felt like a ton of bricks in her rib cage, vibrating from the inside, filling her completely. The bass drum kicked in, resonating up and down her body, and then it was the snare, tightening her skin with each whipping snap. In seconds, they had made her body feel alive with new vigour; only seconds, and the song was at full speed. And just as quickly the whole floor became a soup of thrashing, wriggling punks.

Carlie felt the built-up stress of the last few days leaving her, replaced with sweet distortion and the catchy, aggressive hooks she so loved. She felt herself smiling long before it showed on her face. Letting her heart understand it needed to beat faster, she started moving slowly, but, too antsy to wait, she began dancing full-heartedly, furiously, all much too quickly. The music called for it, but it was also a means to purge. And there was something else she wanted, too. Johnny's advice would need to be ignored; she was chasing it.

She shook and thrashed to the music with desperation, dancing through her lack of breath and dizziness until her blood was properly pumping.

"Come on," she mouthed to herself, cringing with need. Her teeth clenched, she threw downward punches, head slamming, jumping, trying to feel the music, trying to lose control, to lose her grip on what was keeping her heart from expanding.

The music stopped, but Carlie kept moving. If she didn't, her heart would slow down and she would have to get it all revved up again. She jumped up and down, shaking her arms, not caring what others thought of her restlessness. The band didn't linger and followed straight into another tune, one she recognised right away. Her favourite.

"Oh, yes!" She squealed, squeezing her way through the people, with wide, famished eyes. Passing by the body-banging mosh pit, she raised her fist and sang along with them, further electrified by their energy. She reached the stage and, with a mischievous grin, climbed onto it. The bassist, smiling, pointed her to the crowd with his head and the head of his bass at the same time. With his approval, she backed up a few steps, jumped up and down a few times, and ran, thrusting herself over the bodies, where she was caught by a multitude of hands just as the chorus blared its glory. And then she felt it. Like a torrent of water gushing from her pleasure-seeking heart. The blissful threads of lights shot out, bursting with gut-wrenching beauty as she was pushed on her back along the bumpy surface of the dancing crowd like a river raft, the glowing branches of light spreading above her. And she was put down, much too soon to her liking, near the back where she landed firmly.

Eyes shut, she dropped her head and hugged her chest, tears streaming down her face, both in joy and sadness, holding onto the feeling she didn't want to lose.

Carlie went to shows, any show she could, every evening after work. Rock, honky tonk, jazz, you name it. It didn't affect her the way she hoped. Sometimes there was a glimpse of a thread, but it would quickly retreat without having done its job, leaving Carlie more frustrated than at the start of the night.

From the first moment she had felt the threads, the initial contentment of being back home was no longer enough to keep her sprits afloat, eclipsed by the overpowering emotions she now relied on. She wanted more of it, and it seemed to have run dry.

6 Tainted Love

A skunk's tail stuck out from a pile of black garbage bags by the corner store not too far ahead. Carlie clicked her tongue and whistled when she saw it, announcing her presence. The critter poked its little head out from his treasure trove and scurried off.

Skunks were strange creatures. They had way more sway than they thought. They didn't need to eat garbage; they could probably walk into a grocery store and leave with whatever they wanted without anyone stopping them. A skunk was a loaded gun. But, in its unawareness, garbage was safer, and therefore good enough. Carlie was not the type of girl to think that garbage was good enough, and she found herself resenting, if only for a fleeting moment, the skunk for not having the balls to waltz into that corner store and rob it.

It was 2 a.m. Carlie jumped on her childhood BMX and rode in and out of moonlit backstreets. This bike, with its white tires and dirty, peeling stickers. She was happy her parents hadn't gotten rid of it while she was gone. The memories of dirt jumps, races, and skid-mark competitions blew by, whistling in her ears.

Growing up, most of her friends had been boys, and so she had spent nearly all her school years playing what were considered "boy games". Having a big brother as a best friend surely contributed to that, but she didn't mind, mostly because she didn't know any different. As time went by, she realised how lucky she was to have him. The many predicaments he had counselled her out of, and all the times he made sure she wasn't alone walking home, delegating a friend to accompany her when he couldn't himself, all contributed to making her feel safe in an often-unsafe world. And these friends of his had always treated her with respect, because Leo's little sister was not to be messed with.

She slammed on the brakes, slid her back wheel sideways and dropped a foot to the ground. She found herself in a short, dead-end road, lit only by one street lamp she passed about a hundred meters back. The area was full of abandoned textile factories, most of them having gone belly-up eight years ago. Only one little fabric company remained in Moot and had relocated near the centre. *Reggie's Rags*. They served free coffee and doughnuts to anyone who walked through the door.

Still panting hard, Carlie pulled out a folded yellow sticky note from one pocket and a lighter from the other. She brought the flame near it and looked up in front of her. It was the right place. She rolled the bike up against the building's brick wall and gave the seat a loving little pat. The metal door was heavy, requiring both of Carlie's hands to pull it open. Warm air gushed out into the fresh night, a distant thudding from further inside transported with it. Butterflies jumbled around in her stomach in anticipation.

She climbed the steps two by two, up the blue-lit stairway to the third floor. The music was louder, though still muffled, and tempting her from just beyond another metal door. When she opened this one, the drum and bass rushed at her, its clear, unobstructed decibels bringing her utmost delight.

A tall, skinny door girl wearing a multi-coloured shirt smiled her purple-coloured lips, batted her sparkly green eyelashes, and stretched out her hennaed palm. In it, Carlie placed an orange stub in exchange for a raining-cloud stamp, and then turned to face the realm that lay a few steps beyond.

Coloured beams of light flashed through the large, industrial space, exposing hundreds of moving forms in a sea of fake smoke with each sweep. Scattered across the whole area, some were spaced out from each other, while others clumped into what seemed, from afar, like organic entities; creatures and critters, like millipedes, hinged from their articulations. Shady corners harboured more shifting shapes, and their unknown quality called Carlie to them.

Stepping ahead into this warm, hazy world, an infectious energy took over. The music, combined with a unique joy of dancing, shared between each smile, moving limb, and frenzied stare, ignited an impatient urge within her. She neared the stage where the DJ was set up and drifted slightly to the left, facing the speaker where she could feel the wind from the thumping bass against her skin. She began moving her eager hands and feet, letting the rhythm make its way into her. Her heartbeat accelerated, and soon she was flowing, her body fully engaged, upheld in motion by the continuous sound. The buzzing noises, the snare trills, loud crash cymbals, entrancing keys and melodic, booming bass lines all dragged her into a dimension where the only way to dance was with total abandon.

A girl in fluorescent green parachute pants danced her way closer to Carlie. The stranger looked at her with dreamy eyes, a smile on her lips. Carlie smiled back, accepting her in her dimension. With unbroken rhythm, the girl came closer still and extended her hand. Carlie gave hers in return, and a round pill was dropped into it.

"You're beautiful," the girl said in Carlie's ear as she slid away.

"Okay, then." Carlie watched her go, an unjustified ball of affection growing in her stomach.

Not thinking too much about it, Carlie held up the little white pill to her eyes, popped it in her mouth, and kept dancing.

Shivers of pleasure ran up and down Carlie's arms as the sweat trickled down them. She danced, until she couldn't hold her pee in any longer. Her wobbly legs led her across the soft, cushiony floor, bouncing her all the way to the back where an unnaturally bright light illumined a very white bathroom. Some girls stood around talking, laughing and pawing at each other's hair, their clothes a juxtaposition of unnaturally intense colours. Carlie blinked. Behind them a stall door hung open. She slipped in. It had to be the best pee of her life.

Everyone looked happy. Carlie saw short wires of light sticking out of many of them, which pleased her. She knew she was next. She bounced back to her spot, nodding contentedly at the pink and blue lasers flying by. Fresh billows of smoke were released across the floor, and the unearthly place she had been dancing in was now revealed. All the colourfully dressed bopping bodies, she realised, weren't human at all. They were aliens, with beads dangling from their necks and war paint on their faces. All sorts of junk, like stuffed teddies, ribbons, and plastic toys, hung from their belts, neck and hair. Funny species, Carlie thought as she danced. They were friendly, though, and so, obviously, they came in peace. The DJ was an alien too, and clearly he was the leader. A dark lord, perhaps. Carlie recognised his power, how spellbound his people were by his strange, syncopated rhythms, and how he could make them cheer and howl at will. Biting her lip in anticipation, she got as close to him as possible. She, too, was to become spellbound. She dropped her head, closed her eyes, and let her body respond to his control. With perfect timing, the dark lord dropped a thunderous beat. Lasers flew and light threads broke out of Carlie's heart. From deep inside her muscle tissue, she felt them slithering out, eerily, like bone through flesh. Instead of the heavenly tingles she had grown accustomed to, they filled her with a sad, aching longing.

Upon opening her eyes, she saw her threads, beautifully lit, stretching a few feet away. But the ends were charred black and frayed. Her throat closed up when she noticed the DJ's threads which were completely black, reaching out like a hovering circuit of veins, a nest of snakes, wriggling, threatening to strangle whoever came too close.

Carlie stopped moving, a foul taste on her tongue. She watched her wires slink back, the last charred bits squeezing through with a little more difficulty. She placed her hand on her heart and gave it nervous, soothing taps. Inside there, her heart felt more anonymous, more someone else's, than it ever had. A stranger's thread-making machine beat in her ribcage. What craziness. She looked around. The other aliens extruded black-tipped threads, too, and these were all stunted, reaching only a few inches out. They all seemed dazed, staring out somewhere beyond this smoky world. Were they alien *zombies*?

Weaving through the bodies, Carlie's gaze sought their eyes, which, though they looked at her, didn't seem to see her. One step in front of the other, she came to a halt in front of a tall alien zombie blocking her path. Looking up, up into his eyes, she cringed at the white, translucent corneas coating his pupils. A yelp escaped her when she saw them sinking, deep into his head. Diverting her path, she saw that dark sockets engulfed all the aliens' eyes, while smiles lingered at their lips. Carlie hurried. As she forged her path, the bodies grew, taller and taller, much taller than her. Or was she the one shrinking? She skated past the giant, alien zombies as they grew taller still, while she shrank and shrank, until she reached the door. Feeling no bigger than a toddler, she sent a flowery wave of the hand to the multicoloured door girl looming high behind the massive ticket counter.

"Thank you for a wonderful few hours, giant alien friend," she told the door girl in a tiny mouse voice as she exited.

The sun was up by the time Carlie walked up to her house, pushing her bicycle beside her. Someone was sitting on her porch. It was Lucas.

"Oh no," she said from the street. The sight of him made her queasy. She wondered if she should just go through the back door and avoid him completely.

"Carlie." He stood up. "I've been waiting all night. Your brother said you've haven't stopped by for weeks, your work said you were on vacation, and you don't answer your phone. I thought I'd come over to see if you were all right . . . or if you needed anything."

Carlie, suspicious whether this alien came in peace, rolled her bike up to the side of her house and came back out to the front.

"Um, look, Lucas, I had a long night, and I don't feel like talking to anyone right now. Especially not you."

"What? Why?"

"Are you shittin' me right now? Lucas, go home."

Carlie fidgeted with her keys, trying to find the right one to unlock the front door. Lucas put his hand on her arm to stop her. She looked at it, plucked one of his fingers off and discarded his whole hand.

"You don't want me to be happy," she told him without looking at him. "And that's ridiculous."

"No, I do! I do. I have a hard time with giddy people, that's all. Of course I want you to be happy. And I want to be happy with you."

Carlie looked up at him and back at her keys. His good looks were meddling with her thinking. She found the right key and unlocked the door.

"Can I come in?" he asked.

She paused, her hand still on the handle.

"Come on, I've been waiting here all night. I'm tired. I don't want to walk back home right now."

"Fine," Carlie said.

Across the street, a blue Pontiac drove away as the pair disappeared inside.

"Don't ask me to do that again," Damien said, back at Leo's.

"What are you talking about? You wanted to go," Leo answered.

"You're the one who said you had a bad feeling about him snooping back around."

"Ya, so?"

"Well, he was there. The creep. You should have gone. You could have showed up on her doorstep and stopped her from letting him in. She would have listened to you."

"Nah, man. I don't butt in her life that way. You, on the other hand, are in love with her. People do crazy shit for love."

"I didn't even get out of my car. Fuck."

Damien sank into the couch and stared at the black TV.

"You're sleeping on the couch," Carlie stated, throwing a pillow to one end. She placed a light blanket over the couch's arm. Lucas sat at the kitchen table, fiddling with an empty bottle.

"You're not going to forgive me?" he asked. "Look, we haven't known each other for very long, but I like you. I like your soul."

Carlie stopped and turned to look at him. She raised her eyebrows, partly incredulous, partly inviting him to keep talking.

"Look. That night. I was drunk. You were flirting with Damien all evening."

"Uh," Carlie interrupted. Lucas raised his finger.

"We were getting pretty hot, Carlie, you and me, at my place. And you turned off the switch like *that*." He snapped his fingers. "You acted super weird, and I reacted badly. I'm sorry."

Carlie sat on the couch. She leaned her head back and closed her eyes. She was exhausted. Lucas came and sat beside her. Putting his arm around her, he leaned her head onto his shoulder with his other hand and caressed her hair. Carlie, stiff and uncomfortable at first, relaxed with every stroke. She was too tired to be angry.

The sun was blaring through the open curtains when Carlie woke up. She was still on the couch, with Lucas' body plastered to hers. Feeling hot and sticky, she peeled Lucas' arm off and stood up, happy to see she was fully dressed.

"You need a bigger couch," he said in a scraggly voice.

Carlie didn't answer. She walked straight out the door and sat outside on the front porch steps. The street was empty, but the birds were wide awake, as if they were still partying from the night before, having not gone to bed at all. She wondered what time it was.

Lucas came out with two coffee mugs and sat beside Carlie. He handed her one.

"The birds are nuts this morning. They sound so happy to be alive," she said.

"They probably are."

They sat quiet for a while, listening. Putting his cup down, Lucas reached out, placed his hands on Carlie's cheeks, and guided her face towards his, holding her there until her downcast eyes finally flicked up. Satisfied, he tenderly kissed her mouth. His lips brushed against hers, taking off only to make contact again, over and over. Emotionless, she watched him, his eyes half shut, a small frown at his brow. Poor Lucas, she thought. He was like a stupid, broken bird who didn't know he was broken. He just needed a bit of mending. Her pity softening her, she joined in the kiss, still cupping her coffee between her knees. Lucas pulled away, humming in delight, as one would when tasting something delicious. She looked at him, a sad tug in her heart, and the corner of his mouth pulled up in a smile.

"Beautiful," he said.

7 The Good Shit

Carlie peeled off her clothes. The morning was hot and humid, and the shower's water set to cool. She inspected the space between her breasts, looking at her large scar. It was completely healed over, with little bumps where the skin had covered the staples, but without cracks or holes for some strange filaments to come through. She massaged her fingers a little to the left, in the meat, over her heart.

She thought she should feel guilty, about the heart. Someone had died, and, through that death, she got to live. She should be remorseful for stealing the heart from someone else, for not doing anything better with it, something that made her worthy of having it. But she didn't. Perhaps that made her a bad person. She wasn't sure. She also should have written that thank you letter by now.

The heart I have received is magical. It's freaky, but it's oh-so-good. Thank you so much.

Alas, she wasn't going to do that either. Instead, she wallowed in her confusion. Never, before the accident, had she experienced such amazing, inexplicable things. With her own heart, she had known love. Magical in its own way, but with regular ups and downs. Some things had taken time.

"Don't you love me back?" Johnny said, holding her in his arms on the dock, the crashing waves spraying all over them. She answered, her face in his chest, her hands tucked into his hoodie's front pouch.

"I do. I just need more time."

His proposal was refused. It took three years for her to say yes.

She thought about Lucas. She felt no emotion for him.

Maybe she just needed more time.

The phone rang. Carlie tucked the corner of her towel in the wrap around her body and answered.

"Wow, she's back!"

It was Leo.

"Ya, man, I'm alive."

He could feel the smile in her voice.

"So, when can I see you? I miss you," he said.

"I start work again tomorrow. Can you take today off?"

"Sure thing. I'll swing by in an hour?"

"It's a date."

They drove west onto the highway, and up into the mountains. They listened to some punk tapes, mostly, until he popped in some Sarah McLachlan. Carlie gave him a surprised grimace.

"What? She sings like an angel," he said.

He pulled off the side of the road and drove onto a small path cleared of trees.

"Dude, your car."

"It's fine."

He parked in the middle of the path.

"Off-roading?" said Carlie.

He grinned, hoisted himself into the chair she had pulled out for him, and wheeled away. Carlie followed with a blanket and a bag of goodies.

The rest of the path was covered with wooden planks and led to a small clearing by the edge of a cliff where only a few skinny trees obstructed the view.

"Oh! You can see the whole valley!" Carlie exclaimed. She inched her body to the edge and peeked. "Holy crap, it's high."

She spread the blanket. Leo lowered himself down and sat with her. They munched on cheese and crackers and drank some root beer.

"You remember when I was a kid, when you sent me to the store to buy root beer to make ice cream floats, and the idiot clerk at the corner store wouldn't sell it to me because he said there was *beer* in it?" Carlie said.

"Ya, of course. What a moron." He popped a chip into his mouth. "You remember the time when you saved all the school frogs from dissection?"

"Ya!" She chuckled. "I filled four pillow cases of them! Set them loose into the creek near the old mill, and Mr. Gordy was there, walking his dog. You remember him? He hadn't seen me empty the bags and couldn't understand where all the damn frogs were coming from. It was so funny. His dog was *freaking* out."

"You got detention *and* an award from the earth club. Mom and Dad didn't know whether to be angry or proud. They were so confused."

Carlie giggled, then fell quiet. She cleared her throat.

"You remember when I ran away, to get you back from Poptart?"

Leo swallowed down hard, caught off guard. Carlie looked at him, shame welling in her eyes.

"Hey, hey. That's done. Don't," he said, shaking his head.

"I never really apologised. I've always felt too terrible. An apology felt so lame. So useless."

"It wasn't your fault. I was the one driving."

"But you came to find *me*. If I had stayed home, you'd be walking today."

Leo looked away, a small wave of sadness passing through him. After a deep breath, he shook his head again.

"It's done. This is my life, Carlie, and it's okay. And it's *not* your fault."

"Well, I'm sorry, Leo." She looked at him briefly before facing the vast expanse before them. "I wish I had been less selfish. I loved you so much."

She looked at him again. "I still do," she added.

He nodded. "Me too, sis."

They each took a swig of their drinks and looked out at the view.

"So, what's up with the ex?" Leo asked in the most casual way he could.

"Huh? Oh, nothing really. He popped up at the house last night."

"And?"

"And what? Nothing. Nothing happened. I mean, we kissed. This morning, actually. But I felt nothing. I've been . . ." She stopped herself and looked at Leo, wondering if she could tell him about the threads. She would love to tell him. It would be easier to deal with how intense it had made her life if she could talk to someone about it. But he would think she was losing her mind.

"I've been going through some crazy stuff. I can't really explain it," she said.

"Well, you lost your husband. I think it's understandable."

"Ya, I guess." She stopped there, processing the emotions of love and sadness she felt about Johnny.

"I'm sorry. Continue what you were saying."

Carlie sighed, unsure. "Well, at first, you know, the Lucas thing seemed to have potential. We got along well, and he kinda made me feel excited about falling in love again. I know it's really fast, but you know me . . ." She looked into the sky, wondering if

Johnny hated her for wanting to move on. "Anyway, now my heart feels plain dead when I'm with him. So, I didn't think I'd keep seeing him. But then, I was wondering if maybe I should give it time. Maybe my feelings can grow." She looked down, fiddling with the threads from the hem of her jeans.

Leo scowled at her. "Carlie, that's not how love works."

"What do you know?"

"I know that you are way too special, too precious, to waste your time waiting to care about someone who obviously doesn't care enough about you."

Carlie had told Leo about Lucas being a jerk to her the night of their dinner party. He was spared the details, but he had read her face and figured Lucas had done something bad enough. Leo had also been surprisingly pleased to hear that Carlie had been flirting with Damien. She denied it, of course. She felt happy that night, that was all; or so she told him. And then she disappeared, in her chase for bliss.

All around them the birds chirped, hidden in the trees.

"Hey," Leo said. "Don't chase it. If it's meant to be, it'll happen."

Carlie's jaw dropped, slightly stunned by a sense of déjà vu.

"Damien's been worried about you."

"He worries too much," Carlie said, chuckling.

"You don't like him. Did he do something?"

"Are you his spokesperson now? You represent the *Damien* corner?" Emphasising his name gave her heart a weird little tickle.

"No. He's my best friend. You know that. I've known him forever. And he's known you forever, too, but it's different now."

"How is that?"

"He loves you."

Her breath stopped. A squeeze of emotion, and wires of light were flowing, unhindered and easy.

"Is it that shocking?" Leo asked, seeing Carlie's eyes grow big.

"Uh, no. I had my suspicions. I mean, that he liked me. Love, though . . ." She settled into the gentle bliss that coursed through her with a sigh. The threads hovered in front of her without retreating. She flicked her fingers through them. They felt like nothing. Air. Light. No heat. No fuzzy feeling on her fingers. All the feeling was within.

They talked about other things after that. Work, cars, music. All the while Carlie wondered how the threads made their way out, and stayed out, so effortlessly. And how sweet they felt.

"Hazel and I are expecting," said Leo.

Though she tried to hold onto the happy feeling that had monopolised the last hour, Carlie couldn't help her face from falling. The only memory of childbearing she knew came flying back. Leo knew where she had gone in her mind.

"It's hard for you," he said.

She watched the threads pull back, finally. It was only a matter of time before they did anyway.

"No, that's great," she said, pushing her messy emotions aside. "You're going to be a daddy, Leo. I'm going to be an auntie."

She crawled over and plopped down beside him, squeezing him in her arms. They watched the sky change colours in silence.

After that morning, Lucas called her every day, and she told him the same thing every time. "I'm sorry." Three small, pathetic words that combined in such a way gave him the upper hand, or so he thought, because it made her the culprit, and invited him to not give up. As long as she was "sorry" about them breaking things off, he had a foot in the door. So even though she kept swatting him off, he kept bouncing back like a ping-pong ball. This became routine for the next few weeks. The rest was good, though. The job, the free time drawing at the park on sunny mornings, and her visits with Leo. She dropped in at the shop almost every day. Damien was on vacation, and it strangely pained her to not see him. It was for the better, she thought. She had no idea how she would act around him now.

Her nirvana threads, as she had fondly named them, had gone into hibernation. They hadn't come out since her picnic with Leo, and, as sweet as they were, she had no intention of trying to coerce them again. Still, she saw them everywhere. Couples, parents, and children, they all had them. She was sure to come across them at some point during the day, reaching out from someone in their unique, mesmerising way, always seeking something. Though she really wanted to stare, she would look away, keeping temptation at bay, but also choosing to give the person the privacy of his special moment. She wondered what it felt like for them, and if it compared to what she felt. If it did, she wondered, would that not mean she had been doing it all wrong before? As if it was her old heart that was broken. But she couldn't believe that. It had to be different.

It was a slow few weeks of smooth living. Nothing seemed too dull or too intense. And that was okay. The siblings had many suppers together along with Hazel, who was just beginning to show.

"Are you scared?" Carlie asked. They sat on the back deck under the shade of a weeping mulberry tree.

"Kind of. But mostly I'm happy. I love this little worm-kid so much already, it doesn't even make sense to me." Hazel tapped her belly bump with her fingers. "Leo told me you lost one," she said.

Carlie pulled a one-sided smile, her mood darkening. She looked into Hazel's eyes and wondered what kind of magic brewed while the other human grew inside her.

"I was about a month in," she replied, looking down at her child-less belly. Hazel reached out for her hand, and Carlie just stared at it. She wasn't used to girls being nice to her. She was always a little too rough around the edges to fit in with her own gender. Perhaps it was from hanging with the boys so much growing up, or, as a teen, her low tolerance for the drama, the gossip, and the back-biting that seemed to be the result of their flocking together, which was practically absent amongst the boys. So she hung with them instead, or her brother, or Johnny, and girls were just humans she didn't care much for. She had always assumed it was reciprocal since they didn't usually attempt to make friends with her.

But here was this green-haired pixie with a surplus of kindness to offer. And Carlie, older now, and in a new head space, dared to accept it. She let Hazel and her weird fairy-sweetness in.

There were tickles, almost like a forewarning, in Carlie's chest, and then the beloved lights made their way out. And with them, the beautiful bliss. A lump grew in her throat. At once she understood what triggered the lights.

She squeezed Hazel's hand.

"Thank you," Carlie said, now with a full smile. A tear raced down her cheek.

"Aw," Hazel said, her own glowing threads flowing out as she moved in for a hug.

"What's going on here?" said Leo, rolling in.

The girls let go of each other, a new warmth pulsing between them.

"Ah, you know, girl stuff." Carlie shrugged. "Hey, the Ds are back soon."

"And that's making you sad?

"No, but I'm wondering if I'm going to stick around when they are. Things are going pretty good. I think I should move on with my life."

Leo squinted, trying to figure her out.

"Things are going pretty good because you're here. It's good to have you *here*. It's good for me, that's for sure."

He looked at Hazel and pointed towards the kitchen with a nod. "I think the food's ready," he bluffed.

Once she was gone, Leo turned to his sister.

"You can come live here if you want, sis. Not a problem. We'll hook up the basement into a studio suite. It has its own front and back doors. You can have total privacy. If that doesn't suit you, we'll help you find a place."

She didn't say anything, only stared at her hands resting on the table. He rolled closer.

"I don't want you to go."

She pursed her lips and looked up into his loving grey eyes. They seemed so wise.

"I'll think about it," she assured him.

8 Sweeter Than Heinz

It was a sunny morning. The cool air swooshing through the windows filled the house with the smell of blossoms and fresh-cut grass. There wasn't anywhere she needed to be, so Carlie puttered around until she flopped into the living-room armchair with the raggedy Kerouac novel Leo had lent her. She hadn't even flipped the first page when a knock came at the door.

Carlie grunted out of her sprawl and went to open it. It was Lucas.

"Crap," she said.

"Hello to you, too." He smiled, attempting to let himself in. Carlie held the door, blocking the way with her arm.

"Can I come in?" he asked.

"No."

"I'd really like to talk."

"I'm sorry, Lucas, you're not coming in."

"It's all right, Carlie. I just want to talk. How about we talk out here then?"

"Well, I can't. I'm busy."

He looked her up and down. Jogging pants and bra-less under her tank top, barefoot.

"Come on, Carlie, stop playing games."

"I'm not playing games, Lucas. We're done. I'm—" She stopped before she could say the words he expected to hear. A vintage blue Pontiac drove up and parked right across the street.

"I'm . . . expecting someone," she said instead.

"What?" he said, a disgusted pucker at his lips. He watched her eyes fixate onto something behind him. He turned to see Damien stepping out of his car. Damien stayed where he was, hesitating. Carlie's heart beat faster. She gestured for him to come.

"Ya, um, Damien is here. He's going to help me with something. So, thanks for stopping by."

Damien reached the pair and stood beside them on the porch.

"Hey," he said to Carlie, his eyes locked on hers. "What's up, Lucas?" he added with a nod in his direction, without taking his eyes off Carlie's. She dropped her hand from the door. Her stare travelled back to Lucas as Damien walked in sideways through the space beside her, his eyes brushing over her skin as he passed, his body barely grazing her arm but enough to send sputters of pleasurable pain through her heart. She stood paralysed on the threshold, facing Lucas who watched on with a touch of revulsion.

"Nice," Lucas said. "That was predictable. Just thought maybe you'd put on some clothes when you're receiving guests. Or, what am I saying? Of course not. Never mind."

Carlie watched him walk away. She couldn't move, frightened. She didn't care about Lucas, or his insults. She was afraid of what awaited her inside. What she would say. What Damien might say. What she might feel. She was already lightheaded.

Unlatching her cramped fingers from the doorframe, she shut the door and turned, rubbing her hands together. In the armchair was Damien with the Kerouac. He looked up and smiled. Sharp spikes of emotion jabbed at her heart. It was an exquisite pain.

"Great timing," she said, trying to shake off the spell.

"Ya, I hope I wasn't interrupting something important."

"Au contraire." She sat on the couch. "Maybe he'll leave me alone now."

Damien couldn't hold back his smile. He looked down at the book. "This is a classic." He turned it over in his hands.

"I haven't read it yet," Carlie said. "I was just about to start. Leo lent it to me. Says I'm missing out."

He flicked his gaze up from it, and back down. Carlie noticed only now how green his eyes were. She thought it funny how quickly a person could change in someone's eyes. For better or for worse. Though with Damien she felt it had been a long time coming. She pointed to the kitchen.

"Help yourself to whatever you like, okay? I'm just gonna throw some proper clothes on."

The tank top pulled off in one sweep, she lunged onto the unkempt bed in search of her bra. Threading it on with speed, she jumped into some faded jeans, rummaged through a drawer, and yanked out a crumpled t-shirt. She held it up; it was her black Iron Maiden one. She looked at it hard, and then smelled it. As if it could possibly still smell of campfire. The memories stormed in.

"I'll sell you my guitar for five bucks," said the dude playing the guitar.

"Deal," said another guy.

"I'll give you ten," Johnny chimed in.

"Deal," said the dude, handing over the guitar. "Hey, Jenny, let's go to the beer store!" They walked away from the twangy six-string now being plucked by Johnny in the brazing glow of the bonfire. He was wearing the Iron Maiden t-shirt, and a red ball-cap pulled on backwards. He glanced at Carlie every few minutes. She sat on the other side of the flames with some big dude named Heinz. Heinz was built like a wall. Johnny only knew of him—that he was a few years older than them and already in college, liked sports, hockey in particular, and had family money. He saw Johnny looking over.

"That dude is getting on my nerves," Heinz said to Carlie, sitting on the log beside him.

"Who?"

"That dude, with the guitar."

"Oh, Johnny? Why?"

"You know him?"

"From school. He's nice."

"Nice? Okay," he chuckled. "I guess I don't need to worry then."

He wrapped one arm around her waist and lifted her onto his lap. His face was lost under her hair as he kissed her neck. Carlie looked over at Johnny.

He strummed the guitar and sang the words of a popular Green Day song, staring at her as he changed the lyrics, grinning. "Christie Road" would henceforth always be "Carlie Road" for her.

After that night, he always seemed to be near. He followed her around at school, during breaks and at lunch time, easily spotted if she sought him out. Perhaps he had been a lurker before that, and Carlie had just never noticed. But now she did, and Johnny knew, always anticipating the moment when her eyes would find him. It had become strange to leave with Heinz, who came to pick her up at the end of the day, and to know that Johnny was somewhere watching. She began thinking of him, a lot. Then she found the note.

"Whatcha got there?" said the one girl Carlie could stand, Jean. "A note? You in grade two or somethin'?" She chortled. "So, who's it from?"

"Um, none of your business."

Carlie giggled, shoving the paper into her pocket.

"How *uncool*."

"I know," Carlie said. She closed her locker door and followed the herd towards the stairs leading to the second floor for class.

Once Jean was engulfed in the crowd, Carlie darted into the hallway to the left of the stairs. The bell rang. The hall emptied itself of its last few late kids. Carlie sneaked behind another set of stairs and into a storage room.

Inside was pitch black. A moment went by when all she could hear was her own panting, riled up with mischievousness. Then she heard another breath.

"Carlie," he whispered. She didn't answer. Her hands looked for him in the dark. There was the clanging of a bucket or some other junk at her feet as she stepped forward.

"Shit," she whispered.

"Ah, it is you," he said.

"Who else would it be?" Her hand discovered his shoulder and she pulled herself up close to him. She still couldn't see anything.

"Can you see anything?" she asked.

"No."

"Good." Her hands felt their way to his face. She pulled herself closer still, and backed up just enough for their noses to stop touching. They breathed each others' breath in the blinding dark. Her heart raced, thumping loudly, and she was sure she could hear his when they finally kissed. His body stiffened, and then relaxed. He wasn't brutish like Heinz. He was sweet, his touch gentle.

She was wearing his Iron Maiden t-shirt when she left that closet.

"You okay, Carlie?" Damien asked through the door.

Carlie shoved the t-shirt back in the drawer and pulled another one out, pushing her arms through the sleeves just before he snuck his head in.

"You've been in here forever. I made myself a mock-turkey sandwich. What is that shit? It's pretty awful. Anyway, I caught the end of an episode of the *Antiques Roadshow,* and even started reading your book. Well, started re-reading," he said with a wink. "I thought maybe you were hiding from me."

"No, not at all. I'm sorry. I kind of zoned out. Come in."

"I'd rather not," he said, smiling as shyly as Damien could. He didn't quite have the inhibitions to keep his embarrassment from showing, as if it wasn't something he should try to hide. It was endearing.

"Oh." She wondered if it was because it was a girl's room, or because it was *her* room.

Despite his refusal to enter, he looked around, smiling at the Jawbreaker and Fugazi posters. His eyes landed on the bed, the sheets strewn about, the comforter on the floor. Also on the floor was teal underwear, a black hairdryer, a basket of magazines, a set of keys attached to a small plastic Smurfette, and some loose change. Damien sighed.

"You're going to leave, aren't you?" he asked.

Carlie smiled lopsidedly. She had told Leo she'd think about staying, and she meant it.

"I don't know yet."

Damien nodded, accepting the answer as he continued to scan the contents on the floor from the safety of the threshold.

"Let's get out of here," she told him, getting up. She opened the door wider and walked past him, grabbing his hand on the way.

Across and down a few streets was a large, empty field. They flattened down some tall grass at its centre with their feet, the blanket they laid down ballooning over the unyielding blades. When they sat down, the grasses around them were high enough to almost completely hide them from view.

"It's like a fort!" Carlie exclaimed. She pulled from her backpack a thermos of coffee and two mugs, a bag of plain chips and some mint chocolate. They sipped without speaking, their eyes furtive. Damien cleared his throat.

"So, Carlie, what's wrong with you?"

"Huh?"

"What's your flaw? You gotta have one."

"Pfffsh. Is that what we're doing?"

"Come on, name one."

"That's easy. I'm too selfish."

Damien shrugged. They drank some more, listening to cawing crows not too far away.

"How's your heart?" he asked after a while.

"I don't know. Okay I guess. I didn't really care about Lucas anyway."

"I meant your transplant," Damien said, correcting himself. But he was happy with that answer.

"Oh, crap. Ya, of course. Well, it's fine. I still wonder who in the world cursed me with it."

"Why would you say that? That person saved your life."

"I know. I've just been having a real weird time with it. I can't really explain. You'd think I was nuts. It's not all bad, though. I mean, it's just overwhelming. It's so . . . susceptible."

"A susceptible heart? That doesn't sound so odd."

Carlie lay on her back, walled in by the grass and the clear blue sky. She waited for a bird to fly over.

"You are truly a unique specimen," Damien said from his corner of the small blanket.

Carlie smiled, letting the warmth of his words sink in. He couldn't have chosen better words with which to flatter her. Infinitely better than being told she was pretty or some ordinary crap like that. The bird didn't come, so she flipped onto her side and rested her head in her hand, her elbow digging into the soft earth beneath the fabric. She observed Damien for a while as he messed around with some green sprigs in his hands. He had the build of Heinz, but not as square, and Johnny's sweetness, but more manly. He really was like a teddy bear, with his short beard, and those bright, green eyes.

"You are too," she said.

"Ha."

"It's true. You're *Damien*, the one and only." She emphasised his name again. She loved the sound it made in her mouth, and the squeeze it gave her susceptible heart. A frown and a smile grew simultaneously on her face as she played with the patterns on the blanket, avoiding his gaze now that he looked at her.

"I don't want to make you uncomfortable, Carlie, but I've been meaning to tell you something."

Carlie bit her lip. "I know." She still didn't look at him.

"No, wait. I've been trying to find the right time. It's been real tricky. What with the ex-boyfriend creeping around."

"Damien," she interrupted.

"What?"

"Maybe you shouldn't."

"Why?" he asked.

"Because I don't know if I can deal with it right now. My feelings, they're kind of unpredictable. Things seem to get overwhelming pretty fast."

Damien didn't mind those words. They sounded more promising than not.

"Carlie, let me just speak. Please."

"Fine."

"Your brother's going to have a baby. He needs you. He'd never say it, but he does. It makes him so happy to have you back. He's a better person with you around."

Carlie nodded, listening.

"As for me . . ."

Her dark lashes flicked up, her eyes finally meeting his. She didn't want him to say it, yet she hungered for it.

"Well, I'm in love with you. Fully," he said. "But you knew that, apparently."

Carlie stared at him. She hadn't wanted to hear it, but now that it was out, she welcomed the delicious rush of butterflies, throwing their tiny, spark-spraying punches inside her torso. As she savoured the sensation, beautiful multicoloured threads of light responded in turn, piercing her shirt, the strength of her emotion extending them with speed.

"Oh, shit." She sat up as she watched them reach for Damien, surprised at how fast they moved. The lack of control she had over them was unnerving.

Damien sighed, thinking he'd been brushed off again. But, stopped an inch from his own heart, were Carlie's threads. She kept her eyes on them, worried they would drive right into him. Because she felt her heart yearning for just that.

Damien realised she was not getting up to leave. A wave of heat brushed over his skin, and his own threads burst forth, joining with hers in a weave of light.

9 Rendezvous

Damien took a deep breath, stretched his neck to look over the grass, trying to see if there was anyone around. There wasn't. The magnetic pull he felt was tremendous; it urged him to get closer to her, in every way. And he wanted to comply. The sky had become overcast. A cool wind had picked up. He searched for an anchor, a way out, scared to mess things up.

Watching his eyes wander the field, Carlie wondered if he did not feel the same ecstasy she was trying so hard to contain, their threads intertwined as they were.

"I should probably go," he said. His lights pulled back from hers.

"What?" burst Carlie.

"It would be wise."

"Wise? Why would you want to be wise?"

"You're a tad wild, Carlie. I love that about you." He plucked off some grass from his pants, rummaging for the right words. "But, you're up here for me." He made a mark with the side of his hand a foot above his head. "I want to treat you that way."

"Do you treat all your girlfriends that way?"

Damien looked at her with deep questioning in his eyes. He didn't seem to take any of this lightly. There had been Margaret. He was practically married to her for ten years, having begun dating during the last years of high school. A sweeter boy than one would normally find at such an age, he had loved her dearly from the start. Some four years ago, Margaret had run off to Europe with a guy from Westbrink, a city a few hours' drive east, and Damien hadn't received any news from her since. Broke his heart quite perfectly.

He wanted to be careful with Carlie, but not so careful as to scare her away. He never did find out what he had done wrong with Margaret.

"Oh." She realised by his look that there'd been no one since Margaret. She knew the story, but—although she had probably met her in the past, considering Damien had been around Leo since forever, and as a result around Carlie as well—she didn't remember her at all. It would have made sense to judge her badly for her actions. Yet Carlie could understand how irrational a heart could be.

"I've always had love for you, Carlie," he said. "You were family. *Leo's little sister*. I never thought of you in any other way, because I was with Margaret. Not to mention, five years seemed like a big gap back then. But now that we're older, five years is nothing. And you're not just Leo's little sister anymore. You're *Carlie*. I really didn't expect . . . when I saw you again . . . that it would give new life, a *different* life, to something that was already there."

Damien figured he'd talked enough, thinking his touchy-feely banter might just be the thing that would scare her away.

It didn't. Though love and lust were very confusable things at times, Carlie knew there was a delicious blend of them being crafted between Damien and her, thanks to years of friendship and a newly discovered attraction, both physical and photonic—if one was to attribute to the light threads their own elemental properties. Their own desire, of sorts. Deciding very naturally not to resist the magnetism she felt, Carlie crawled towards him. He watched her, his heart racing. She got close enough to feel his quick breath against her face. It smelled of coffee and mint. Her threads, smooth and fluctuating, hovered between them.

"Could you give this susceptible heart a chance?" she whispered, dropping her gaze from his eyes to his mouth.

"Carlie . . ."

She placed her arms around his neck and kissed him before he could say anything else. He breathed in her warmth with thirst, finally tasting the lips he had been dreaming of. His hands moved as if they had a mind of their own and grabbed her exposed waist, pushing against her hips to keep her at a distance. He kissed her without rushing, savouring it, his love for her bubbling to the surface of his skin. His threads burst out and entangled with hers, sending a rush of sparkling emotion into both of them. Their lips became eager, but still soft, their tongues sweet like candy. Damien kept his hands firmly on her hips.

As much as his senses were overwhelmed with desire to pull her in, he would not allow her any closer. So she leaned into him as far as she was permitted, falling into their kiss, her feelings for him more intense than she had imagined, her enlivened body held a safe distance away.

The blanket was folded and the mugs packed up. All the chocolate had been eaten and the bag of chips was empty. The clouds had thickened, early afternoon feeling like evening.

"It's gonna fall," Damien said.

"We should hurry."

They jogged back and reached Carlie's place just as the thunder clapped, dropping its heavy downpour seconds later. They sat on the bright pink rectangle under the porch's roof and watched the curtain of rain drench the streets.

"Well, *I'm* already confused," Carlie said.

"What with?"

"Us."

"Don't. Let's just take our time with each other. You hold back if you need to, emotionally. I'm okay with that. Me, my heart is done for." He looked at her, and then back at the rain. "But I need to hold back physically."

Carlie fiddled with her thumbs.

"Is there something wrong with you?"

"No," Damien said, choking on an uncomfortable laugh. "It's just . . . This . . . *you*, are too important. I don't want to screw it up."

"I'm not exactly sure I understand."

"We'll figure it out. I gotta go." He turned to her and stared for a moment into her clear, brown eyes, and then leaned in to touch his lips to hers. He stood up and, hunched as though it would keep the torrent from soaking through, walked up to his car and disappeared in the rain.

Carlie went inside. It seemed very empty, suddenly, and silent. She grabbed a banana from the counter and flopped into the arm chair with the Kerouac.

Her mind kept wandering back to the field, to Damien, reliving everything that had coursed through her just a few hours before. She could see his face on page two, taste his mouth on page four, feel the tight grip on her hips on page ten. She would never get through the book this way.

"What's this doing here?" asked Johnny.

"What? The book?" Carlie joined him.

"Yes, the book. You never read in the bathroom."

"Ah, but you do! I think it's following you. It wants your eyes on its pages. You wouldn't want to hurt its feelings."

Johnny shook his head and sat down with it on the side of the bathtub.

Johnny read a few lines and looked up from the page. "This corrupted and rotten body? It's not starting off too well. I'd prefer to just re-read *The Little Prince*."

"Dude, Siddhartha." Carlie raised her eyebrows convincingly, to which Johnny shook his head again. Carlie yanked the book out of his hands before trying to push him into the empty tub.

The phone rang. Kerouac lay on the floor, under Carlie's dangling arm. She rubbed an eye with her other hand and looked around. The sun was setting. She would be late for work. The phone kept ringing. A pang of pain pinched in her chest, so she rubbed it. Ring. The armchair was trying keep her hostage. She wriggled away and, still rubbing her chest, stumbled over to the phone. The answering machine picked up.

"Darling, it's your mother. We're catching a flight out of Rio tomorrow night. See you soon." Beep.

Elbows on the counter, head in her hands, Carlie pushed her hair back, stretching the skin of her forehead, forcing her eyes to open wider.

"Crap," she said. After speed-brushing her teeth, she grabbed her backpack and ran out the door.

At work, Carlie thought about Damien. She couldn't understand why a thirty-year-old guy was already acting like an old man, wise with prudence. A puritan almost. Carlie was twenty-five, old enough to make responsible decisions, she thought to herself. Though she knew she often didn't.

She wiped down some tables mindlessly as her thoughts drifted again to Johnny, and at how easy it had been with him, physically and emotionally. They were both in their last year of high school when they hooked up. Young, wild, and free. Carlie never felt as though she had to make sacrifices with him. Everything just flowed. They had their arguments, but were always back to normal in a matter of hours. Perhaps there was no challenge because there was no growth, she thought. And the thought felt like betrayal. He had been the most caring boy ever, the best thing that had happened to her, really.

A harsh pain struck Carlie in the chest again. She bent over, her hands on the counter and her head hanging between her arms.

"You all right?" a customer asked, a twenty-dollar bill in hand.

"Ya, thanks. I'm fine."

She handled the transaction, unbending only slightly.

"Bon appétit," she said, as he walked out the archway into the restaurant.

Jolts of pain shot through her body, the light threads bursting out a few inches each time, bringing a strange, sputtering pleasure into the mix. Over and over again, the stabbing pain struck in her chest, and the threads flared through her curled fingers clutching her shirt, only to slip back inside a second after.

It was supposed to be a numb heart, they said.

Anxiously waiting for her shift to end, she struggled to keep it together. The last few customers, oblivious to her, had no plans of eating and just sipped their drinks until Carlie finally kicked them out shortly before closing time. She couldn't take it anymore.

She rushed out under the bright moon, jogging most of the way, stopping occasionally to deal with the pain and the awful thuds each heartbeat sent into her head.

The frequency of the jolts spaced out, and, by the time she got home, the pain had mostly subsided. Her bag dropped to the floor, the front door flung shut with the heel of her foot, Carlie went straight to her room. Exhausted, she resisted the temptation to dive into her bed and drown in her blankets. Instead, she rummaged through her stuff. Papers, clothes, photographs, and jewellery flew.

"Ha!" she said, taking out a business card. Her appointment had been last week. She had missed another one two weeks before that, and another two weeks before that. She'd missed them all. A hot flash pushed beads of sweat out of her skin. She walked to the phone. Her fingers tapped the countertop nervously as it rang.

An emergency check-up was scheduled for the next morning. The pain could be normal, the nurse at the other end of the line had said. Dizziness, fever, vomiting, and shortness of breath: those were the things she had to look out for. Those were signs of an infection. She didn't have any of those symptoms, and still took all her meds daily. That was pretty much all she was supposed to do, all she could do, except eating well, exercising, and perhaps showing up for her check-ups.

There would always be a risk of her body rejecting the heart. Carlie knew this. It would be understandable, she thought, if her body didn't want it; it wasn't hers.

"Good morning, Miss Jones," said the doctor when Carlie came back from the room where the blood work was done.

"Good morning, doctooorrr . . ."

"Mayet." They shook hands before Carlie sat down in front of her. The office was meticulously clean, with modern, squarish metal-and-wood furniture. The walls were the unfortunate off-white she had no affection for.

"So, you like playing with fire. You missed all of your three scheduled appointments," said Doctor Mayet. She looked at the questionnaire Carlie had filled out in the waiting room. "And you took psychotropic drugs, but you don't know what kind or the dosage. You know that's dangerous, in any case, but especially for you. It could have seriously conflicted with your medication. You also could have triggered a form of psychosis, or overdosed. It could have been a one-way ticket, Miss Jones." The doctor shook her head.

Carlie twisted her mouth to the side, looking down at her dirty sneakers. Her jeans had holes in the knees. She should have dressed nicer, she thought to herself. She felt like a bum.

"I'm sorry I didn't come to my appointments. I felt fine, so I kind of forgot," Carlie said. "As for the drugs, I know it was a stupid move. I really wasn't being careful. I was trying to make something happen."

"And what was that?" the doctor asked.

Carlie wished she had held her tongue a little better. "I was trying to feel something . . . something powerful."

Carlie stared into the grey, low-pile carpet at her feet, making small fists with her hands as she remembered. When she looked back up, doctor Mayet had at least four new creases on her forehead. Carlie had to admit it sounded pretty desperate, as if her life was empty without whatever feeling the drugs could bring her. She couldn't tell this woman about the threads. The whole thing was insane enough to have her committed.

"Are you feeling depressed, Miss Jones? Is that why you took the drugs?" the doctor asked.

"No, that's not why."

"How are you coping with the death of your friend?"

"Husband," Carlie corrected. She thought for a moment. "I feel surprisingly better, actually."

"Oh, any reason you can think of?" Clearly, prying was part of her job.

"I loved Johnny, and I will always miss him. I'm not sure I believe in heaven or anything, but I feel like he's still around, helping me to heal, in a way. The pain of losing him isn't gone, of course. I don't know if that'll ever change. But I think . . . I think I found love again."

The doctor's resulting smile was comforting, like a parent's approval. Once Carlie assured her she wasn't having any symptoms other than the recent chest pains, the doctor gave Carlie another set of pills to take. She also gave her a bit more crap for her reckless behaviour and sent her off to get changed for her biopsy.

She lay on the operating table, a place she didn't particularly enjoy, and the catheter was sent down her vein into her heart. She had had these procedures before, and she was looking forward to the day she didn't have to have them anymore.

"Okay, it will feel like I am tickling your heart," doctor Mayet said. Carlie liked how she said it was *her* heart. It was in her body, was it not? The idea of keeping it was growing on her.

The catheter was moved around, intentionally bumping the little snippers at its end against the walls of the heart's inner chambers. It didn't tickle as the doctor said, but it didn't hurt either. Only a strange, distinct feeling of a poke.

"Just looking for a sweet spot." She concentrated. Finally, a sample of tissue was snipped off.

Carlie wondered if the nirvana threads showed up on the screen. No one said anything, so she assumed they didn't. They would have surely pulled out the hazmat suits and quarantined her for life.

The catheter was pulled out painlessly.

"We will be calling you soon with the results, Miss Jones," said doctor Mayet, taking her leave.

Carlie dumped her crumpled blue hospital robe in a laundry basket right outside the door. She'd be happy as long as she didn't have to come back right away. She hated being at the hospital, possibly why she had "forgotten" her appointments. These halls, though different, felt exactly the same as those she had found herself walking down just a few months ago; and by virtue of their likeness, they held memories they had no right to.

10 Trust

The low afternoon sun illumined the oil-stained floor, a long shadow stretching from Carlie's feet as she walked in through the rolled-up door. Leo popped his head out from behind a car in the back.

"Hey, sis! Give me just a minute."

Damien heard, put his tools down and walked out to her. Unsure if a night's sleep had changed her feelings for him, he stopped a step away.

"Hi," he said.

Leo rolled up. He looked at Carlie and at Damien, and then at their hands. Carlie let go and shoved her fists into her pockets, her pinkened cheeks hot. Leo grinned.

"So, uh, Leo," she said, "Mom and Dad are flying out of Rio tonight. They'll be here tomorrow morning. I'm going to pack up." She pointed over her shoulder with her thumb.

Worry washed over his face. "And, where are you gonna go to?" He rolled a little closer. Damien looked uneasy, eager to know the answer as well.

"Is your basement suite still an option?"

"You betcha! I'll make sure it's ready by tonight."

Carlie giggled, jumped into his lap and kissed him on the cheek.

"Thank you."

"Knock, knock," Damien said, poking his head in. Garbage bags of clothes blocked the door.

"Oh." Carlie ran up to move them. She opened the door and backed up amidst the other bags and boxes scattered on the floor. "I'm sorry. Come in."

"I hope it's okay I popped by. I figured you might need some help. Plus, I wanted to see you."

"Of course, it's great, thanks. I wanted to see you, too."

"Oh yeah?" Damien asked, intrigued, and then worried. "Why?"

"Just because, silly. You've been on my mind."

"That's good to hear." He smiled, and then looked at the mess. "So, what's your system?"

"I'm emptying my old room, properly. These boxes are to take to charity. The bags at the door, too. These boxes I will keep." She pointed around the living room at the half-filled boxes.

"What can I do?"

"Bah, just talk to me."

"Okay." He moved a box full of newspaper-wrapped, mystery items from the armchair to the floor so he could sit. A hardcover black book with some worn out stickers on it had been hiding underneath. He plucked it up as he sat, holding it up for Carlie to see.

"Oh, my sketch book," she said.

"May I?"

"Sure."

Black ink drawings of superheroes, three-eyed animals, and robots made out of household items peppered the pages.

"This is awesome." He turned the book to show her the drawing of the trash can with Mickey Mouse arms riding a skateboard. He flipped the page and fell on a drawing of her living room as seen from above, with a man on the couch, her couch, holding the hand of a girl. He knew it was him, his Yankees ball cap clearly detailed, and Carlie, with her dishevelled morning hair, plaid pyjama pants, and whale tattoo well depicted.

"Whoa, this is good. I remember that day," he said with slight discomfort. "What's with all the black hair coming out of my body? 'Wires of light again. This time out of Damien,'" he read the scribbled note underneath the drawing. Dated the day it happened, June 3rd. Carlie stopped moving when she heard her note being read.

"What's this, Carlie?"

She kept her head down, her eyes on whatever was in the box in front of her, afraid to look. Could she tell him? Would she scare him away if he found out she was a freak? She wasn't ready to lose him; she had just got him.

"You're gonna think I'm crazy," she said. Damien shrugged. "Seriously," she continued without looking at him, moving things from one box to another. "I haven't told *anyone*. I would get locked up in a loony bin."

"Holy smokes, Carlie, relax. What are you talking about?"

"You don't understand. I really think that if I tell you, there's a big chance you'll think I'm on drugs, or psycho, and you won't want to be with me anymore, and you'll tell Leo, and then he will put me in an asylum."

"Carlie, you're freaking out. I assure you that won't happen. But look, you don't have to tell me if you don't want to."

"Oh. Okay then. Good."

She went into her room and came back with a handful of stuffed toys.

"Okay, I changed my mind. You gotta tell me," he said. "This is too intriguing."

"Fuck. You're smiling, but you shouldn't be. I'm telling you, you're gonna think . . ."

"Just spit it out, will ya?"

The teddies and doggies and dinosaurs dropped to the ground. Carlie stared at him. It would be good to tell someone. But she was terrified to do so.

"To hell with it." She legged over a row of boxes and sat on the floor in front him.

"When I told you I was having a hard time with my heart being *susceptible*, this is what I was talking about."

Damien closed the book and placed it carefully on his lap, giving Carlie his full attention.

She took a deep breath.

"At first I didn't understand what triggered it, but I've narrowed it down to intense, genuine feelings of passion or love. Not necessarily romantic love. It can be between friends, or between a mother and child, for example."

She looked up at Damien, who, though he listened attentively, was still clueless.

"I see lights."

She waited. No reaction. She continued, "I see *threads* of light. They can be different colours—usually yellow, green, or blue. Sometimes white. They come out of people, Damien. They come out of their chests. Their hearts, specifically, I think. I say heart because that's where I feel them when they come out of me. The other thing is that, when it does happen to me, it's overwhelmingly good. Physically, emotionally . . . It's the most amazing thing I've ever felt." She smiled to herself. "So, it's not a bad thing, at all, I think. It's just really . . . out of this world. I don't know why this is happening."

Damien listened, nodded, keeping his eyes on her as she spoke, her own gaze now on her fidgeting feet.

"And this drawing?" He pointed to the sketchbook in his lap. "That day you freaked out when I held your hand . . . You saw these light things coming out of *me*?"

Carlie's eyes, wide with fear, met his. She gave a small nod.

His lips pressed tightly together. He shook his head. "I don't know what to say, Carlie."

Tears welled in her eyes. Her throat tightened.

"Hey," he said. "Come here." He moved the sketchbook and tapped his thigh. She crawled into his lap, burying her wet cheeks in his neck. He wrapped his arms around her waist.

"I'm not going anywhere, okay? Whatever this is, it doesn't scare me. We'll figure it out."

"You don't think I'm a freak?" she mumbled.

"Of course I do. But who cares? It sounds like a pretty cool hallucination, if you ask me. Did your mom drink while she was pregnant with you?"

Without pulling her face out of his neck, Carlie give him a little slap on the chest.

"So, does it scare *you*?" he asked.

She sat up straight and sighed, relieved and slightly incredulous at how cool he was being.

"No, not really. It's beautiful to look at, and it feels divine. Like, when we kissed . . ." She turned to look at him, their faces close.

"Yes?" He wet his lips.

"Well, my lights, and your lights . . ." She stopped, distracted by his mouth. She felt her threads sleek out, snaky and smooth, and, though she could also see the glow below from his, she kept her eyes on him.

"After our lips finally met," she continued in a whisper, "our lights collided, tangled, and twirled around each other. It sent jolts of pleasure through my whole being."

The rising and falling of Damien's chest came faster. His eyes on Carlie's lips, her warm breath lured him in, making his mouth water.

She inched closer.

"Is this what it feels like for everybody? Have I just been doing it all wrong before now?"

"Doing what?"

"Everything."

Her parted lips touched his. His tongue reached for hers, and she gave it to him. Their threads followed, sweeping Carlie over with intoxicating emotion.

"I love your mouth," she breathed through the kiss.

"I love you."

Carlie's hands found their way under his shirt, the feeling of his skin making her more impatient.

"Mmm. Okay, okay." Damien tried to pull his face away, putting his hand over hers to keep them still. "Whew. Okay. We should really get back to packing, ya? Your brother is expecting you."

Carlie nodded, remembering his wish to keep things slow. She took her hands back.

"Are you ever gonna get naked with me?" she asked.

A visual of their intertwined bodies flashed through his mind.

"Carlie, don't do that to me."

She giggled and got up, ready to finish packing her life.

11 One Step Forward, Two Steps Back

The next day, Carlie woke up in her new apartment. It would do the trick, for as long as she needed. There was plenty of light, for a basement suite, hanging plants colouring every corner. Her half-dozen boxes and two bags of clothes were unpacked and placed before morning was over. From the backdoor there were stairs that led up to the yard where Leo and Hazel invited her to eat every day, and which she almost always accepted. She saw Damien nearly every day, too, and, after a short week, was already getting used to the ease with which her threads came when she was with him. Even from just holding his hand or looking at him, the threads would be involuntarily summoned, along with the beautiful feeling that came with them. She was floating, high on love.

As he became more important in her life, the daydreams of Johnny became less frequent, and, although she still missed him, she didn't feel as much pain when he did visit. Sharing her secret with Damien seemed to have created an openness that softened her grieving at the same time. A burden had been lifted.

"That lady," she said as they walked down a small neighbourhood street, pointing to a tall, skinny woman waiting to cross the road.

"The one with the miniature collie in her arms?" Damien said. The dog wore a little pink vest and seemed extremely pleased with it too.

"Yes, her threads are bright green."

"And what are they doing?"

"They're wrapping themselves around her dog."

"Nice."

When Hazel sat on Leo's lap and kissed him, when they made eyes at each other, Carlie would lean over to Damien.

"Yellow. And blue."

"What about ours?" Damien asked once.

"They've become rather white-ish," she had said.

Carlie's parents had been surprised to come home to an empty house, and even more surprised to see her room cleared out except for the bed and dresser. They were back for the month of August and then leaving again.

"So how's your summer been, dear?" her mother asked from across the table. She and her parents were alone in the bungalow that day, and this was the first time they had seen each other since they got back. The mood, no more than lukewarm, yanked at Carlie's ankles, trying to pull her down from the cloud she was living on. Her toes were already touching the ground by the time they began passing around the Chinese take-out containers.

"It's been pretty interesting," Carlie answered, accepting a Styrofoam tray of rice from her dad. "I've been working at the Cave. It's not a career, but it's okay for now."

"So, since it's not a career, as you say . . . Have you thought about our proposition?" her mother continued.

"I did, actually. Going back to school sounds . . . good."

Carlie's parents both straightened up, exchanging surprised glances and restrained, pinched smiles.

"Don't be so shocked," Carlie said. "It's a really sweet deal. Thanks for offering to pay. It's hella generous of you."

"It's our pleasure. We just want to see you make good choices, Carlie. This will help you thrive."

"Have you chosen a field?" her father asked.

"Yup. Fine arts."

Disapproving grunts echoed over the screeching of Carlie's fork. She threw an undercooked piece of stir-fried broccoli in her mouth and chewed hard, swallowing it too fast. She knew it wouldn't go down well with them, just like the vegetable stuck in her throat.

"Wouldn't you want to choose something that would provide you with more financial security?" her father asked, gesturing with his chopsticks.

Hand on her throat, she reached for her glass of water, closing her eyes to block out her parents' stare as she drank, forcing the uncomfortable broccoli down her oesophagus. Wiping her mouth with the back of her hand, she opened her eyes to them waiting for a reply.

"I'll do an extra two years of teacher's college, and that way I can work as an art teacher. Is that better?"

They both nodded, satisfied.

Her apartment door barely open, Carlie heard the phone ringing. The keys still in the lock, she ran to pick up. It was the hospital.

"Oh, hello," Carlie said. Dr. Mayet's voice was on the other end of the line. "Oh. Sure, I can come by. At four? Okay."

She hung up and went back to the door to retrieve her keys. Suddenly dizzy, she started down the hallway, tilting, catching herself on the back of the couch as she passed it. Her hands firmly planted in its velvet, she held herself up, blinking hard. The floor teetered beneath her feet, her mind a porthole onto a windy sea.

But it subsided, and short moments later she was standing straight. On solid ground, she headed for the shower.

"The tissue analysis shows that your body is trying to reject the heart," said Dr. Mayet from her damn ugly beige office.

Carlie did not fail to notice how the doctor said *the* heart this time, instead of *her* heart, as she had done before.

"Your prograff levels—the anti-rejection drug—are normal, but it seems to not be working sufficiently well. We will need to give you different, stronger immuno-suppressants, in hope that your body will stop trying to refuse the new organ, and extra drugs to combat the possible side effects. Everything else seems to be fine, Miss Jones."

Everything else seemed to be fine, apart from her body rejecting the heart.

As it was, they said, about seventy percent of heart transplant patients lived at least two years after surgery. The ten-year survival rate was closer to fifty or lower. What if Carlie only had a year and a half left to live? The thought nagged at her as she took the long walk back to town from the hospital.

About an hour later she arrived at the garage.

"Hey, Leo," she said, giving him a fancy handshake with slaps and snaps.

"Hey, sis."

"You sound awful. What's going on?" she said.

He let out a huge sigh and looked over into the closed corner office, the one they never used, with the large glass windows on two of its four sides. Inside, Damien was talking to a girl.

"Who's that?" Carlie said.

"That's Margaret."

"What? No." Frowning, she screwed her eyes towards Damien, trying to read his facial expressions. He seemed worried. Margaret was moving her hands a lot. She saw her take a step closer to Damien, and he opened his arms for her.

"*Why* are they hugging?" Carlie said.

"I don't know, Carlie. But she's bad news, that's for sure."

Damien finally came out of the office, followed by Margaret pushing a stroller. Buckled in was a chubby, sleeping baby, drool leaking down his chin. A blue blankie dangled over the edge and dragged on the dirty garage floor.

Damien's eyes widened when he saw Carlie.

"Hey, Carlie," he said, pulling her aside once he got to her. He gave Margaret the just-a-minute finger.

"What's going on?" Carlie asked.

"That's Margaret. She just showed up here. She's in trouble, kind of. The baby's daddy left her."

"And? She wants you to take his place?" she said, letting out a nervous chuckle.

"Something like that. It's ridiculous, obviously. But I have to at least hear her out. I owe her that much."

"What do you mean, owe her? *She* abandoned *you*, heartlessly. You owe her nothing," Carlie said, purposely loud enough for Margaret to hear.

"Yes, but, when she left"—Damien lowered his voice—"she was pregnant with our child, and she got an abortion because the other guy wanted nothing to do with it. I just found this out. I had no idea."

Carlie's eyes kept jumping from him to Margaret as she processed what he said.

"What does that change? This is not your kid," Carlie whispered, mirroring his tone.

"But it might as well be. We were supposed to have one."

"You do know that's not how biology works, right?"

"Ya, well, she had no right to destroy that baby without telling me. I'm kind of pissed, actually," he said, looking over his shoulder.

"So, what are you saying, Damien? That you might get back with her?" Carlie shifted legs, tapping her fingers on her crossed arms.

"No, no. Of course not. I'm with *you*." He paused, looking into her eyes. "But Margaret and I were together for a whole decade. I can at least listen to what she has to say, in a better setting than here. We're going to have coffee and chat right now. I'll call you later."

He kissed Carlie, who was too stunned to speak, on the cheek. Waving to Margaret, she followed him outside with the stroller and the dirty blanket.

Leo approached Carlie, looking as worried as her. She lowered her glassy eyes.

"Hey, hey," Leo said. "Don't worry. She did so much damage to him, he'd be insane to take her back. Anyway, that won't happen. You are literally his dream come true. He can't stop talking about you. It's kind of weird, you know, since you're my little sister, and he's my best friend, but it's real cool at the same time. You guys are great together."

"Ya, well, I hope you're right. And thanks." She kissed him on the cheek and headed out. She forgot to tell him about the heart.

She meandered through the streets, taking useless detours, prolonging the time before she'd be home with nothing to distract her from the many ugly truths that were threatening to guillotine her happiness.

Inevitably, she got there. Throwing her backpack on the couch, her feet dragged her to the kitchen area a few steps away. She pulled out a pot. Opening the tap, she filled it with water and put it on the stove to boil, standing over it until it did. Tiny rings of bubbles—shrimp eyes. Ropes of pearls. Raging torrent. A drop of oil and a box of spaghetti dumped in, she stirred. And stirred. She flung a noodle at the wall. It stuck. She left it there. Straining those in front of her, she placed some on her plate, drizzled some more olive oil. Sprinkled some salt. She sat at the table. Her fork twirled the pasta into a small nest. The reapings were shoved into her mouth. She chewed. They tasted fine. But the quiet of her apartment was sneaky. It smuggled thoughts in through the back door, ushering them through with every disjunct move, every bite, until she realised: she was crowded in. Her chest tightened. Her face flushed with heat. The unwelcome worries wouldn't be pushed back out, and she had no fingers to stick in her ears from the inside. It was too late.

Damien was presently somewhere with his conniving ex-lover. Maybe they were in his apartment, alone. Maybe eating, as she was, or just sipping drinks. Maybe they were sitting close to each other, too close; and Margaret, maybe she was reaching over to touch Damien on the knee, maybe drawing circles with her finger on his jeans. Maybe they looked at each other a little too long, awakening a forgotten longing. Maybe. And it hurt Carlie to think about it, but the fact was that whether or not Margaret won him back, Carlie could be losing him anyway.

The first tear escaped down her cheek, leading the way for all the others. They flowed with every squeeze of her heart, running over her lips, dropping from her chin and onto her food. She heaved as she ate, concentrating on chewing and swallowing to avoid choking, until she put her fork down and wrapped her arms around her belly, breaking into sobs. She'd lied. In that hospital bed, she had lied. She didn't want to die.

12 The Poem with the Mostest

Maybe her time was up. Life had tried to off her once and failed. She had cheated her way out of what had been destined for her, cheated her way out of death. Survived, despite the bigger plan of things—those things written out in the invisible blueprints of the universe. Like how long it takes for a seed to germinate in the right conditions, or at what time in its life a caterpillar changes into a butterfly. Just maybe, it had been her time to moult, to change states, and pulling through had been a mistake enabled by overly competent doctors, by one heart-recipient dying too quickly, and by all the unsuitable bodies ending up in code-blues, called out loudly in the intercom for all to hear, and seen rolling by on sheet-draped stretchers with weeping family members in tow.

And in this way, they mistakenly gave the heart to Carlie.

But Carlie was in love. And falling in love with Damien couldn't be a mistake.

If she did anything right with her new heart, that was it. And the magic that it blessed her with couldn't be a mistake either. A glitch in the space-time fabric, perhaps, or some other, inexplicable phenomenon. It didn't matter. The nirvana threads had become a guide, a thrill, something to look forward to, a testament to her passion.

Morning came. Tears had encrusted Carlie's hair to her face. Her swollen eyelids, opening with difficulty, exposed the same messy life she had fallen asleep to. Her feet struggled out of the blanket wrapped around her limbs, off the couch and onto the cold floor. With an in-breath, she pushed herself up from the sinking cushions, the springs creaking as she rose, and dragged her bare soles with dry, swishy noises all the way to the bathroom.

"Ugh," she said, seeing herself in the mirror. "You look like shit, Carlie Jones."

Wrinkles from the crumpled-up shirt she had used as a pillow had left a Kandinsky of criss-crosses on her left cheek. She avoided her bloodshot eyes, resisting the dreaded honesty that she'd find there, brushing her teeth and washing her face with her gaze set on her nose or chin. She brought herself up close to the mirror, opening up her puffy eyes as widely as she could to apply some mascara. She focussed on her lashes, and, finally, just stared herself in the damn face.

It was pretty bad. She wasn't sure if it was the brown of her iris that was browner, or the black of her pupil that was blacker, but that morning her eyes looked like bottomless pits, with no light to be found in the soul they housed. She was still staring, mid mascara-motion, when the phone rang. She ran.

"Hello? No, I don't want your Kirby. Leave me the hell alone." She slammed the receiver down. "FUCK."

A knock sounded on the back door. It was Hazel.

"Good morning, Carlie," she said. "We'd like to invite you for waffles. Also, Leo wants to make sure you are okay."

"That's really sweet of you guys. I'm not really hungry. You can tell him I'm fine," Carlie said, forcing a smile.

"Supper, then?"

"Sure, thank you."

She finished in the mirror, treating her features like those of someone else, and left without bothering to change out of the clothes she had slept in.

Her take-out cup beside her, the morning was spent on a wooden bench in a tiny park only ten or twelve feet wide, tucked away between a few houses lining a narrow street she had never explored before. Carlie was perfectly hidden. And without, so far, any people or cars passing by on that lazy Sunday morning, she was perfectly alone.

Her coffee tasted bland, just as any food should have on such an occasion. She drank it as a means to an end, and as something to do while her heart fell apart, figuratively and literally. She needed to keep her mind off Damien, and off death. Breakfast with Leo would have been brutal.

The plastic lid to her lips, her eyes hopped around as she sipped. A long crack zigzagged in the sidewalk just beyond her patch of grass; a crust of dead bugs contoured the edge of a lamppost's yellowed bulb cover; a Boston fern, bursting with leaves, filled a small window of the house across the street, probably its bathroom; and the window beside it was pasted in coloured shapes, cut raggedly with the skill of a small child. Aground, a few small branches, leaves and dust spun in a small twirl of wind, and, further, a ball of paper skidded down the street, pushed by a different finger of the same breeze. She followed it with her eyes as it came closer, tumbling and grazing the ground, sounding just like Carlie's dragging feet did earlier that morning. It hit the edge of the sidewalk and flung upward onto the grass where it continued bouncing straight towards her. She plucked it from its path. Holding the crumpled piece of paper by an edge with one hand, she observed it as she took a last sip of coffee from the other. She placed the empty cup beside her and opened up the paper, flattening it on her thigh. There were only five lines, written in an old-fashioned cursive script, slightly faded by the explosion of creases.

To the one who seeks,
Find within, yet transcending all
The mysteries of sacred Love.
Guard thy heart, for in it lies
The undying light of all creation.

What a strange offering. Looking up into the clouds, she took in the inked words. How meaningless they could have seemed a few months before, and somehow rich with parallels now. Impressions of how they related to her existence sailed her mind, passing through in waves. Like tiny suns of understanding bursting at the crest of each ripple, the longer she sat with the words, the more intense became her clarity. And then, quite suddenly, as if stepping out of a cold sea, Carlie felt wide awake, washed clean of the dirt that had been pulling her down.

And, just like that, the park she sat in became richly saturated with colour, brought to life with a snap, the edges of everything she saw sharply defined. Everything popped out as if to say: "You've never noticed me. Look, I'm a crazy-ass green blade of grass"; or "Check out my sharp bark ridges, bitches." As Carlie drank it in with a gasp of air, her surroundings snapped again, the colours now even richer, and her vision so keen she could see the particles that made up that crazy grass, and that sassy tree, and everything else; a sea filled with trillions of tiny tapioca balls. Carlie sat still with her eyes wide. Too alert to be dreaming, she felt as though a constricting membrane had burst inside her head, giving her more room to breathe, to think, to be.

The quivering tapioca balls seemed to be held together by something magnetic, like invisible jelly. A jelly that knew where to place each of the little tiny balls. As if it were . . . intelligent. More than that, she felt desire pulsating from it—a deep want to exist, to have its gazillion tapiocas lovingly arranged in its particular way. As real as she was, sitting there in the park, so it seemed that all was held together by that loving desire, and all was correspondingly ephemeral. As volatile as an idea.

The more she stared into the simple canvas laid out before her, the more she began to see them: the particles stretched out into minuscule nirvana threads, dancing and tickling each other through the jelly. Miniature versions of her own, these worms of light permeated everything, the building blocks and also the mortar of all she could see. Her hands. The space between her fingers. The tree a few feet away. The empty paper coffee cup. The gust of wind that picked it up, just as she observed it, flinging it into the air, and out into the street where it rolled away amongst more of the tight, wriggly threads that made up the world.

She looked down at herself. Not an inch of her was without the lights, slithering and bright. She felt her arms swelling, though when she looked at them saw that they weren't. And she felt her chest taking up more and more space, though it stayed the same size. Her skull, opening, widening, gave way for the pressure within it to expand even more, seeking the limits of space. Large and permeable, she felt as if she could have fused with her surroundings, or floated away beyond the stratosphere, disappearing either way if only she chose to. The peculiar bodily sensations weren't without sentiment; a deep inner peace anchored in her heart, which throbbed with a rare, new sort of love. Immersed in a pervasive harmony, she felt in tune with everything, reminiscent of her state of mind after she had woken up from surgery.

A stranger appeared, walking along the sidewalk that lined the park. His body motion was fluid, squiggly lights bouncing around his swinging arms and long, striding legs. His eyes, dark and serious, landed on Carlie. This man, she wondered, was he as awake as she was right now? Could he feel that he was just an arrangement of particles, just a jumble of light? Could he feel the strange love in him that she felt in her, and in everything around her? He pulled his gaze away from hers and sped by without looking back.

After a while, the threads began dissipating, and her oversized energy shrank back into her tight muscles and bones.

The chill of the wind brushed her bare neck and brought her back into the concrete reality of the morning. She peeled off the paper, still draped on her thigh, folded it neatly, and pushed it deep into her pocket.

Death. That was what Carlie mulled over on her way home. The poem said a heart's light was undying, and she wondered if there was any truth to that. If she never did anything important, or meaningful, and didn't live on in people's memories, wouldn't she just be forgotten? She imagined her dead body feeding the worms of the earth, and her soul, feeding the light threads in a similar, decomposing way. Perhaps that was how one endured.

"Here she is," said Leo, opening the door for his sister that evening. His eyebrows tweaked into a questioning frown. "You on something?"

Carlie bent down to hug him and sighed. Standing back up, she stared at him, her eyes dreamy.

"Nope. That would be bad for my heart." She walked over to Hazel to collect her hug. Leo followed her to the table.

"Carlie, you look seriously keyed up. What's going on?"

Carlie sat down, smiling. Hazel stood behind her and dished some steaming, roasted sweet potatoes onto her plate.

"Thank you, Hazel," Carlie said. "I've had an intense last few days, Leo."

Hazel sat down and gestured to the other bowls on the table before serving herself some green salad.

"I went to the hospital yesterday," she continued. "They told me my body is rejecting the heart."

Hazel gasped. Leo's face hardened.

"They gave me a bunch of different medication." She reached for a bumpy-looking veggie burger. "They'll be following me closely. But there's a chance that it won't stick. You know, there will *always* be that chance. It's not my heart, so . . . It's more like *it's* rejecting *me*, and not me it. Did you know, a heart can beat on its own for a while, if you take it out? For a fleeting moment, it is its own entity. Pretty cool, huh. During a short glimpse, in all eternity, it needs no one. And then it dies." She squirted some ketchup onto her open bun. "You know, we're all going to die." She burst into a hearty, genuine laugh.

"You're trippin'," Leo said.

Carlie grinned, holding the mustard bottle.

"I promise I'm not. I'm thoroughly, utterly sober. If anything, I feel more awake than I've ever been."

Hesitant, he released his frown, and put food on his plate.

"Do you believe in God?" she asked him.

He dropped his utensil to the floor with a clang.

"What? Stop talking crazy, Carlie. You're not going to die." He reached down to pick it up.

She thought of telling him about the poem, but she felt it was more like a secret love note, like Johnny had given her once upon a time. And love notes one keeps to oneself. If Leo mocked it, it would surely stifle the sweet high she was enjoying, though all the mockery in the world wouldn't change what had happened in the park.

"Have you heard from Damien?" Carlie asked between bites, looking at Leo, then at Hazel. They shook their heads.

"That's okay, I guess," Carlie said, a slight dip in her sunshine mood. "I'm sure he'll do what he feels is right. He's a real good person, you know."

"Yup, we know," Leo said.

He and Hazel looked at each other from the corners of their eyes, worried by Carlie's easy-going mood. Perhaps she was in shock. When she was ready to go home, Leo followed her all the way to his door, watched her walk out onto the back deck, u-turn once on the grass, and finally disappear down the steps that led to her suite. He rolled around and flung the door shut with a flick of the wrist.

"We should keep an eye on her," Hazel said.

"Something's up, that's for sure."

13 Sacred

A knock came at her door. Green tea steaming on the coffee table beside her, Carlie was sunken in the couch, curled up with her Kerouac and too comfy to move. But she knew it was probably Damien. As cool as she felt earlier about whatever decision he'd make, she was nervous now. It could be over between them, without her even knowing it yet. With a deep breath, she pulled off the thin old blanket covering her bare legs and walked across the small living room in her oversized sleeping t-shirt. The knock came again before she got to the door. In the shadow cast by the upstairs' porch stood the source of possible joy, or sorrow. She let him in.

"I'm sorry I didn't call," Damien said, stepping inside. Carlie smiled at him, reminding herself of her experience in the park, of how much love there was to be felt, whether or not Damien was by her side. She walked back to the couch and climbed under her blanket. He closed the door, standing beside it for a few seconds before sitting at the other end of the couch. A long moment passed before he spoke.

"Margaret's ex is still in Europe. She is going to Westbrink, to look for his parents, to see if they want to be part of their grandchild's life and help her out. She's kind of a mess."

"Oh." Carlie imagined if Leo wasn't around how her own parents would react to a green-haired Hazel showing up on their doorstep with a baby in her arms.

"And where are her own parents?"

"Dead."

"Oh," she said, with more empathy this time.

"Listen," Damien said. Carlie's breath stopped. "You don't need to worry. I told her I can be there for her as a friend. That's all."

Dizzy with relief, she blew out the air she was holding. Damien was not going to be anyone's knight in shining armour but her own. She knew that was selfish, but she didn't care. She loved him. Telling him about her failing heart was going to be hard.

Damien watched her fiddle with her old blanket, poking her fingers in its many holes, testing different ones until they fit through.

"This whole thing got me thinking," Damien said.

"Ah ya." Carlie stretched a hole wider as she forced the tip of her index finger through it.

Damien lifted his bottom off the couch to reach into his pocket and pulled out a small black box. He turned it around in his hands and looked at Carlie, his lips pinched in a tight smile. She watched him, waiting for the next string of words to come. He flipped the box open.

"Marry me?"

A few sparkles came off the ring as the light hit it.

"What?"

Damien lowered his head. Her reaction made his heart sink just enough to show on his honest face.

"I love you, Carlie. It's not complicated. I know this is fast, but it feels nothing if not right. I feel like I can honour you properly this way. I can honour us." He looked at the box.

Johnny had asked for Carlie's hand many times before she accepted. It was strange how the men in her life had the need to get married. No one else she knew seemed to have that problem.

"I'm a widower, you know. I've done this before. I can tell you, it doesn't change anything."

He nodded. "I'm truly sorry about Johnny. It's horrible what you had to go through. I think, though, that he would want you to be happy. That's what I would want for you, anyway, were the tables turned. I don't know the circumstances of your marriage, or what he believed in. But I think marriage is between souls first, and bodies second. It makes a bond sacred."

"Sacred." The word resonated within her. "You're more spiritual than I thought."

Damien shrugged. "I think love is a spiritual thing, before all else. Does that freak you out?"

"Not at all. I think I believe that, too." After the kind of mystical experience she'd had earlier that day, she was pretty convinced that love was the most powerful, intangible force there could be. That was the best definition of *spiritual* she could think of.

Damien, a little more hopeful, turned the open box over in his fingers until it faced Carlie again.

"I'm really happy that Margaret hasn't messed things up for us," she said. "I know you're a caring person, Damien. It must have been hard to tell her no."

"Actually, it wasn't." Leo was right.

"I have to tell you something." Carlie shifted around in the caving couch to sit up straighter. "My body is rejecting my heart."

Guard thy heart, she remembered. From what?

Damien frowned, his green eyes darkening, the corners of his lips tugging downwards. He faced ahead.

"I could die," she said to him. "There will always be a risk, at any point in my life, of this happening. And, it could be soon." Sorrow filled her as the words left her mouth. Death didn't scare her, strangely. What she found herself grieving was the future with Damien she might never have.

The box, and the silly trinket inside it, hung between the tips of his fingers. He stared as the window curtain lifted from the wall and fell back, as if breathing, inflated by the incoming breeze. He closed his eyes.

"I'm going to make you a tea," Carlie said, touching his knee before she struggled to get up.

His eyes stayed closed until the whistling of the boiling water called him back. Carlie put down the steaming cup at his end of the coffee table and sat beside him. He placed the little black box beside it, and, with his freed hands, invited her closer. She rested her head on his chest. He had a strong, steady heartbeat. One that would last much longer than hers, most probably. He smelled her hair and laid his cheek on top of her head.

"I'm here for you, Carlie. For as long as you want me. The rest, we can't control." He pulled away to look at her. "I still want to marry you."

Carlie took a deep breath.

"Do you want to be with me?" Damien frowned. Carlie didn't have to overthink before she nodded. He continued, "You know me, Carlie. And I know you. If you want to be with me, I'm here."

Sacred, he had said.

"Okay," she whispered, raising her head.

"Okay?" Damien's face lit up, his smile wide. She nodded. His smile then loosened and fell. He reached for the box, pulled out the ring, and lifted Carlie's hand as if it was a fragile baby bird. She giggled as he slipped it on her finger. He looked so serious.

"Damien?"

He narrowed his eyes at her, looking almost angry. He didn't say anything. He just stared hard. But he wet his lips, and Carlie's heart faltered. She knew he wasn't angry. With his stern frown, he moved in closer. Butterflies fluttered up and down her core, painfully climbing up to her heart. As he pressed his mouth on hers, a sort of frenzy overcame her. The fear of losing him, and the rush of relief that she wasn't, combined with her feverish lust for him, all burned under her ribs, violently bursting into bright, voracious snakes. Damien's were right there to catch them.

Desire and love were not the same. She knew that. But they were a perfect pair. Two hands to one body. Like Damien's hands, pressing up Carlie's back and climbing up her neck, or hers, cupping his square jawbone and feeling his chest. Enticed by the flowing heat waves pulsing from their joined lights and all through her frame, Carlie pushed herself away from the man-eating couch, swung her leg over him and, with a little of his help, straddled him. She pulled off her night shirt in one swift movement, her long, loose hair falling over her shoulders, covering her only partly. Not enough to obstruct their half-open gazes as their lips were consumed in mouthfuls, nor to cast a modest, concealing shadow on Damien's unabashed and wandering hands.

"I'm so happy," he said, grabbing the opportunity of a soft ebb to speak, combing her hair with his fingers and pulling it forward over her shoulders to cover her bare chest.

"Mmm."

"We ought to cool down."

"Why," she asked, her eyes glazed. She kissed his cheek and pressed his hands against her neck, where they still played with her dark strands, leading them down, lingering on the flesh hiding under her wavy hair, and finally sliding them to her hips. "If I'm not mistaken, we're going to be married. It's legit."

"Well, yes, it will be, after."

Carlie cocked her head and studied him for a second. Her threads began slithering back in as she realised he wasn't kidding.

"You're not kidding."

He laughed, though his eyes were determined.

"Please," he said. "It's hard for me too."

"I would hope so! Dude, you're thirty, you were with Margaret for like, ten years. You weren't married, nor chaste."

"I know. That was then."

Carlie looked down at her ring. It was very pretty. Two small, offset, shiny rocks on a gold band. It was a tiny bit loose. She moved it back and forth with her thumb.

"Sacred," she said.

"Yes."

"Okay, you big baby. But kiss me some more, husband-to-be."

He wrapped his arms around her hips and pulled her in.

14 Evil Threads

Damien left, and Carlie picked up the empty cups, tossing the tea bags in the lidless garbage. She smiled to herself, thinking she had lost her mind, this time for real. She was getting married, *again*.

A stab of pain shot through her chest, followed by a hot flash. With no time to make it to the bathroom, she turned to the garbage and vomited, propping herself up on the edge of the counter and holding her hair out of the way with the other hand. Her face above the receptacle, she waited. The floor was shifting again, and the walls were moving, but the next wave didn't come, and the nausea slowly went away. She felt for a glass, poured some tap water into it and swished it around in her mouth, spitting the rest of the sick into the empty metal sink. The medicine bottles were out on the counter already, so she popped them open and took what she was supposed to; two from two bottles and one from each of the other three. She grabbed a banana muffin that sat on a dish and collapsed in a chair at her dimly lit dinner table, holding back her tears as she ate, twirling her shiny new ring with her thumb.

Daybreak came, looking like night, the sky dark with rainclouds. Thunder cracked just as the phone rang, jolting Carlie awake.

"Hello?"

"Carlie, you're still sleeping?" asked Leo. "It's noon. Come have lunch."

"All right, I'll be right up."

They could hardly contain their giddiness, trying to keep a straight face, pursing their lips to keep from smiling. They wanted to give Carlie a chance to tell them herself, but obviously they had already heard the news from Damien.

"Yes, yes," she said, waving the back of her hand at them so they could see the ring. They shouted and whooped, Hazel jumping into Carlie's arms and Damien waiting for Carlie to jump into his. But she slid into them, calmly and slowly.

"What's wrong?" he asked when he noticed how sluggish she was.

"I'm just tired." She rested her head on his chest.

Leo looked at Hazel, whose giddiness swiftly disappeared. She nibbled on her thumbnail.

"You should lie down," Leo told Carlie.

"I have a shift at four."

"No, you don't. You're calling in sick."

She didn't need convincing.

"In fact, sweet sister of mine, I think you should stop working for a while. You don't need to pay rent, and we'll cover your food. I'm sure Derek and Denise can help too. They were really unhappy you hadn't told them about your doctor's appointment."

"It was just two days ago. I didn't have time. I was busy getting engaged," she muttered, holding onto Damien.

"All right, Carlie. Just remember, they might be distant, but they love you. Anyway, what's important now is that you get better."

Damien led Carlie to the couch.

"Want some TV?" he asked. Carlie didn't answer. He turned it on and found some funnies. Hazel pulled a small blanket over her legs and retreated to the kitchen with Leo where they whispered to each other. They called the hospital while Damien stroked his fiancée's hair.

Both in wheelchairs, Carlie and Leo sat in the waiting room. When the nurse finally showed, it was clear who was the sick one. Carlie's head was tipped to the side, her neck limp with sleep, her face clammy green. She was rolled into the examination room, followed by her brother, while Hazel and Damien stayed behind amongst a few tremulous elderly people and some coughing children attended to by exhausted parents. By the time they came out an hour later, Carlie was sleeping again, and so was Hazel. Leo gently woke her up, and they all headed home.

The next few days were filled with sleep and a lack of appetite. A fever came and went. Damien visited after work, car grease on his face and hands. Carlie liked it. An honest man doing an honest day's work. He would lean down to kiss her where she lay, and her lights would shoot right out, bright, intense, always ready for him. He asked her about it the next evening.

"So, the light threads, are they still around?" He sat on the floor beside the couch. She strained to flip onto her side to face him.

"Brighter than ever." She smiled.

"Really?"

"Ya, but just with you. I'm too tired to feel for anything else." She chuckled, but Damien darkened.

"They tire you?"

"Well, it's intense, so . . . I guess it uses some of my energy, ya." She shrugged.

"Oh." Damien glanced around the room as he thought, ending back on Carlie's face. He looked into one of her eyes and then the other, switching like this two, three times.

"What? Why so serious?"

"Why so serious? Leo told me the doctor called this afternoon."

"Yup."

"They've been analysing your heart tissues. Comparing this time and last time. They aren't really sure what's happening, Leo said."

"Nope."

"Apparently, they said the tissue damage worsened incredibly fast, faster than they've ever seen, and that you shouldn't even be alive right now, but somehow you are."

"That sounds about right."

"Do you think it has something to do with those things?"

"The threads? I've never thought about it."

"She says you should keep resting," Damien said.

"I have been."

"But feeling the threads with me makes you tired."

"Uh . . . I guess, ya."

"Can you control them?"

"You mean like, keep them in? I don't know. Come here." He leaned over, placed his hand on her cheek and his lips against hers. Carlie's body softened as she returned the kiss with a notch more heat. The threads came out and danced their way to him, filling her with well-being. He pulled back and she sighed.

"Mmm, I don't think I can, nor do I want to." Her eyes were still closed.

Damien frowned. "And if I hold your hand?"

"Mmm, lights." She nodded. "I think I love you."

"And if I just sit here?"

Carlie forced her eyes open to glower at him.

"Look," he said, "I don't want to be the cause of you getting worse. You need to get better. You . . . you have to heal. It's simple." He kissed her on the cheek, lingering there a little, and got up. In the kitchen, he exchanged a few words with Leo and took off.

He didn't visit the next day. Nor the next. Sometimes Carlie heard his voice, but he wouldn't stay long, and never entered the living room. Leo acted as the messenger: Damien was thinking of her, he loved her, and he'd see her soon. It was better this way for her, he said. It hurt Carlie, but, after three days without seeing Damien, she was already sitting up, eating full meals, and walking to the bathroom on her own. By day six she returned to her own apartment.

Pink Floyd, the Smiths, and Dave Brubeck kept Carlie company, spinning on the old record player as she took to her sketchbook to pass the time. She listened and drew. Over and over, a super-heroine, heart tentacles flowing like whips, catching bad guys and wrapping around her lovers like a predatory insect. She missed Damien.

"What is it?" Carlie giggled, feeling the present with her hands, her eyes squeezed shut.

"Open it," Johnny said. It was their second "date" since the storage-room incident, and he thought taking her to Pine Beach would be a good idea. He was right. On a blanket laid out in the sand by a large driftwood log, Carlie opened her eyes and unwrapped the small rectangular box, the newspaper wrapper floating off in the wind.

"A mixtape," she said, pleased. He took it from her and popped it into his Walkman. With an earbud each, they lay back and watched the clouds roll by, hands clasped between them.

Her life had been full with Johnny. She had found happiness with him. But he was taken away from her, and in his stead she was given something different. She didn't dare think "better". One could use words, like hot, deep, heavenly, even. But they were just words, and love was just love. It didn't need to be described. Just felt. Its distinct flavours were never the same from one situation to the next, from one person to the other, and so she didn't dare compare them ever again. This was what life had given her. That was all. Life had gifted her a *Damien*.

And this Damien stayed away to keep her passion threads tucked in her heart, where they couldn't suck the life out of her.

15 Sea You Later

Two weeks apart, and she felt almost normal. She took a walk and, though she missed him something fierce, avoided the garage per his request.

"Ah, you're home," Leo said from over the phone.

"Ya, I just got back a few minutes ago," Carlie said.

"Can you come to the back?"

"Sure."

Leo sat reclined under the shade of the mulberry tree.

"You're not working today?" Carlie asked, sitting on a chair beside him.

"Ya, a bit later."

"How's Damien?"

"He's happy you're doing better. Otherwise he drags his feet around all day, a real mope. You ever going to explain to me what this is all about? He says he makes you weak? I think it's total bullshit. But you two seem okay with your arrangement, so . . ."

"I'm not okay with it at all. I miss him like crazy. I hope I'll be able to see him, now that I'm better. But . . . even the doctors tell me to keep up whatever I'm doing. And the only thing I'm doing is staying away from Damien." Carlie leaned her elbows on the table, chin in hands. "I know it sounds messed up."

"Are you sad?"

"Not exactly. I feel empty."

"Huh. He said the same thing. Well, I'm sure looking forward to seeing you two reunited."

Leo unlatched the lock from his wheels that kept him tilted back and straightened out, rotating to face his sister.

"Maybe it would be a good time for me to tell you some good news," he said.

Carlie raised her eyebrows. The shade of the tree made interesting patterns on his face. She smiled at him.

"You're beautiful," she said.

"Okay."

"So, what's up?"

"You left one of your sketchbooks here yesterday morning," he said.

Carlie caught her breath. She laid her hands on the table and stared at the space between them, listening.

"And well," he continued, "I took the liberty to show it to Matt, one of my clients. He works for a big publishing house in Westbrink. 'Brick Tower' it's called. Drives in about once a month. He had an appointment yesterday afternoon, and, well, I showed him. He said if you can come up with a story, he'd love to help you publish a graphic novel."

"For real?" she said, the nervous spell broken.

"Ya! Isn't that absofuckinlutely awesome?"

"Is it? Holy shit! Wow. You took my stuff without asking, though, and showed people. That's . . . not great. But still, wow! Thank you." She shook her head in disbelief.

"He'd like to meet with you next week to chat. He said if you could have something for them to look at a few months from now, you could be published by the beginning of the new year. But I guess he'll tell you that himself."

Spreading her arms, she hugged him and kissed his cheek.

"I gotta go process this. Is that cool?"

"Sure thing. Oh, Hazel stocked your fridge while you were out."

Carlie thanked him and returned to her apartment. She decided to call the garage.

"Vintage Shop," Damien answered.

"Hey you," Carlie said.

"Carlie? Oh, hey. How are ya?"

"I'm doing real good, actually. Sorry to call you at work. I don't want to bother you. I know you said it's better if we don't . . ."

"It's okay, Carlie. You're doing good, and that's all that matters."

"Well, not to me. We matter. I feel empty without you."

"Maybe that's part of the problem."

"What's part of what problem?"

"Us, being too intense. If you could be happy without me . . . If you loved me . . . less," he said.

"What? Whatever, Damien. Bright candles burn fast."

"I can't accept that."

"You said you were here for me, Damien. Were you lying? As soon as there's a bump in the road, you're gonna ditch?"

"It's not like that. This is my way of being there for you."

"By staying away?"

"Ya."

"Well, *I* can't accept *that*." A heavy silence fell, accentuating the buzzing of the fridge, the knell of the wind chimes outside the door, the passing cars. The whispered "I gotta go". The soft click as he hung up.

She swallowed hard, blinking away the tears. The graphic novel, she decided. She would focus on that. It was Friday, and Matt wanted to meet on Monday. Leo offered to drive her but she insisted on taking the bus.

She drew all weekend, sketching up the story of OctoBitch. She needed a better name. It was fitting, though, since the gift of the threads was now becoming a curse. She wasn't feeling warmly about herself and it came out in the character. She had no affection for Lazer Lucy, SnakeHeart Sophie, or Tentacle Tammy, whose names also surfaced. They were all too ridiculous, but, then again, so was the story. A broken-hearted superhero loses her powers when the love of her life, the WrenchKing, leaves her for a normal human, tired of being trapped in her heart tentacles every time they make out. He tells her to use her powers for the good of the world, not to attempt murder every time he tries to love her. Broken hearted, she can no longer wield the inflicting sting of her heart whips that her enemies have come to fear. Taking advantage of her vulnerable state, they catch her and lock her in a dungeon, and ruthlessly take over the city. The WrenchKing catches wind of her capture. Though he left her, he loves her still, and can't bear the thought of her suffering. And so, swinging his giant wrenches in his gigantic arms, he charges out to the fort that holds her prisoner, knocks down the walls and saves her.

Carlie couldn't figure out how to end it. The WrenchKing fears her snaky grip. And OctoBitch, well, she can't help it. Carlie thought maybe OctoBitch could kill the WrenchKing while making victory love. A nice, dramatic ending.

The bus wasn't even half full. The woman sitting across the aisle from Carlie reeked of cigarettes. Carlie imagined the woman dumping her ashtray on the floor and rolling around in the butts. That's how bad she smelled. Carlie wondered how dirty her lungs were, and if this woman would ever be lying on a hospital bed, waiting for a transplant of her own. A half hour in, Carlie walked up to the bus driver.

"So you say I can use this same ticket to get on the next bus in an hour?"

"Yes, dear. At the same spot you'll get off. You wait for it there."

He turned into a rest stop off the highway and opened the side door for her.

A small wooden building sat on the edge of a wide, lengthy strip of grass. On the other side of the grass was Pine Beach.

Carlie took off her shoes. The warm sand squeezed between her toes, wrapping around her heels as her weight sank in with each step. The air smelled salty, though the river had some distance to go before becoming the sea. Seagulls cawed, glided and swooped around each other. Small waves broke on the shore, and retreated, over and over, drawing a meandering edge of seaweed along the limit of its reach. Every element cried out for Carlie to enjoy the rich memories they invoked, and so she did.

Her blanket spread by one the many driftwood logs on the beach, she plopped down with her backpack and pulled out a folded piece of paper out of a small side pocket. Unwrapping it carefully, she once again read the anonymous poem.

To the one who seeks,
Find within, yet transcending all
The mysteries of sacred Love.
Guard thy heart, for in it lies
The undying light of all creation.

She struggled with the last line. She understood that the mysteries of Love were within her, in her own being, and beyond. Beyond the limits of her own self, her own body and soul, her own understanding. She'd seen it through the nirvana threads, but had also felt it through Johnny's love, through music, through art, through family, through Damien. She could see it, with her everyday eyes, in the waves that flowed endlessly, the trees that swayed afar, the gulls that rode the air currents. This was a love that existed despite her, yet she was intertwined with it through her sight, through her hearing, through the burning passion of her heart. It was everywhere, and obvious, and still it was nothing if not mysterious.

Her contemplations filled her with a well-being that soon had her feeling lighter than air. Before she saw their glow, she felt her threads triggered, deep in her heart's flesh. And, for the first time, she felt that she could decide whether to keep them in. With this new choice, she wondered for a moment how wise it would be to let them flow. Though they might have weakened her, and though she expected them to do just that, she didn't want to resist. She would have them do as they would and let the bliss she had been sorely missing course through her. And so they did, and Carlie melted into it as in the embrace of a long-lost lover.

The enigma resurfaced. *Guard thy heart.* If her light was undying, what would she need to guard it from? Darkness could not affect her. Metaphorically speaking, the darkness of others— their judgement, their jealousy, their hatred—could not blot her light, because she wasn't the one projecting the darkness. There was no battle to be fought; by its very nature, light would always obliterate darkness. Carlie thought only she could truly kill her light, through those same feelings of hatred, anger, greed, or by being unforgiving, perhaps. So, she thought, that had to be it. She needed to guard her heart from her own self, and such things as would seduce OctoBitch to the dark side.

Carlie's threads were acting strangely. They didn't just float out to the front and hover as they usually did. They spread out further and further over the water. A pressure at the top of her head, she leaned back to see a thick beam of brightness, shooting out, up past the clouds, beyond what her eyes could see. She looked back down and saw skinny white worms of light coming from her arms and reaching out to either side, far into the vastness of the beach. Meanwhile, her feelings were so strong, so ardent, so divine, she was hardly able to sustain it and thought she might faint.

"It's going to kill me," she said to herself. But she lay on her back and let what felt like nothing less than the light of pure Love gush from every part of her. Her body expansive, without borders of skin and bones keeping her together, it was the park all over again, times a million.

Thoughts of Damien bubbled past. Leo, Hazel, her parents . . . They sailed through, alighting and taking off like feathers adrift.

She had no more attachment to them than she did to the breeze carrying them through. It was paradise, she thought. In its very essence. This was it. Nothing mattered. She could leave everything behind and fly off in this feeling. There would be no sadness. It was perfection. And, in this perfection, no questions remained.

But thoughts of Johnny pushed through, along with her sketches, Matt, and Westbrink. The euphoria wasn't meant to last. Her eyes fluttered open, the dreamlike expansiveness drawing back into the sheath of her body like a sea drained into a cup. It took its time. When she felt solid again, she pushed herself up. Looked at her watch. She had ten minutes left. Her movements deliberate, she folded her blanket with care, placed it in her backpack, and tucked the poem back in its pocket.

The next hour and a half was spent staring out the window. Carlie felt as if she had drunk a hundred coffees, but without the jitters. The thin veil wrapping her mind had once again popped and dissipated, but this time it stayed that way. Everything was crisp, yet soft. She felt in love with it all. She felt absofuckinlutely awesome.

But something didn't add up. If she was strong enough to live through that, how could connecting with Damien possibly be killing her? It was a different kind of love, she thought then. It was beautiful with Damien, but she couldn't fool herself. This was a different level of energy altogether. One where she connected to Life itself, as opposed to a specific person. Maybe the answer was there.

The thoughts, spiritual or otherwise, brought to her awareness at the park through the poem, didn't stick around as she would have liked them to. Clearly she needed to revisit the words to conjure the otherworldly experience. She wondered if there were other poems out there from this mystery author, waiting for her to snatch them from the wind. How could she possibly find out?

She waved goodbye to the bus driver, squinting her sparkling eyes with a smile. He smiled back, seeming touched. The streets were crowded, downtown Westbrink a hub of commerce. Much more so than in Mootpoint, being at least twice its size. People walked in and out of shops. Others lined up before the street vendors' tables to dote over whatever was being sold. Handcrafted jewellery, t-shirts, sunglasses. People loved buying things; new things, cheap things, expensive things, doubles of things. Carlie walked down the main, passing a table of books managed by an older, large lady, her rolls of fat trying to escape the sides of her folding chair. Carlie looked over the books. Perhaps one day one of her own would be recycled in such a way, waiting for someone to lay eyes on it. She crossed the street and entered the tall, stone-clad building on the corner.

The meeting was kept short. Matt was a busy, no-bullshit kind of man. But kind. Carlie could tell by the way his eyes wrinkled when he smiled. He didn't want to waste any time, he said, after looking over the drawings. He loved the OctoBitch idea. Even the title. Copies of the quick sketches were made to keep on record and to show his team. He presented her with a contract, told her to look it over. Now she just had to get to work.

16 An Energy Ground

Carlie got home and went straight to Leo's to tell him the news.
Damien stood in the kitchen with a beer in his hands. Carlie's
heart leapt. She ran to him and wrapped her arms around his
neck.

"I missed you!" she said. "Damien, I had the best day. I have
to tell you about it!"

Damien's smile showed concern. He still thought it wasn't
good to be around Carlie, but Leo had persuaded him to cut the
crap and be there for her. Carlie slid down from his neck and
hugged Hazel, and then jumped into Leo's lap and hugged him.

"Holy huggy bunny, do tell us what happened." Leo laughed,
happy to see her so well. Hazel offered her a beer, to which she
waved her hand and shook her head. She didn't want anything
messing with her natural high, ever again.

She told them about the meeting and shared with them the
story she pitched. Leo and Hazel loved it. Damien, knowing
where it was coming from, didn't think it was so funny.

"You don't like my story, Mr. Moore?" she asked when they
were alone in the living room. They sat on the couch, Damien in

the middle facing the TV, using the baseball game as a distraction. Carlie faced him cross-legged, the couch's arm supporting her back.

"I would if it weren't so close to the truth," he said, giving her a quick glance and puckering his lips as if he had just sucked on a lemon. He sighed. "I'm really happy for you, though. This is really amazing." He nodded, lightening up. He placed his hand on her thigh, and then thought better of it and pulled it away. She watched him.

"I had a mind-blowing experience on Pine Beach." She leaned in closer to him.

"What were you doing there?" This time he turned to look at her. Her face was too close to his. He had almost forgotten how pretty she was, trying so hard to focus on work these last few weeks, trusting that their separation was for the best and that it was better not to torture himself thinking about her. He still did, but the mental picture didn't do her justice. Her dark hair, her freckles, the clear chocolate-brown of her eyes, her full lips. Even her little scar under her ear, on the edge of her cheekbone, was endearing to him. He shook his head.

Carlie thought he was disapproving of her going to the beach alone. "I took a pit stop, for old time's sake, on my way to Westbrink. I understood some stuff, Damien, about what's happening to me."

Damien raised his eyebrows.

She lowered her voice. "I had a *spiritual* experience, Damien, with life, with nature. On the beach. There were threads and beams *everywhere*. I was like a colander of fucking light. And this *love,* like I can't describe, spilled in and out of everywhere. It was nuts! Everything else pales in comparison to how this felt. Everything."

Knowing he came second now, or further even, on her list of intense feelings hurt his ego a little, though that was exactly what he told her he wanted. For her to be happy without him, to love him less. Or in this case, love something more. And besides, he understood. He had had spiritual experiences in the past too, though nothing even close to what she was describing.

"I felt fabulous afterwards. It didn't weaken me at all," she said, all perk. Lowering her voice again, this time to a whisper, she smiled. "I think I know how we can . . . be together."

Damien's head cocked to the side, like an animal twitching its ears to a noise in the distance.

"You might think this is strange, but I think we need to try connecting to each other by going *through* that source, first," she said, her eyes wild. "Like a ground."

Damien had heard plenty of strange things from Carlie since finding out about the threads. This wasn't as far-fetched as the rest.

"You could tell me you discovered how to time travel and I think I'd believe you. You are so convincing right now."

"So, yes?"

"It's worth a shot."

"Awesome!" She was pleased at how open-minded he was being. She knew he was in tune with his own soul, which would surely help them. She leaned closer still. "So, you know your way around the *Source*, do you?"

"Small yes and a big no. I don't think anyone ever does. But you seem to have something extremely special going on. You're lucky, I guess. I trust your intuition, Carlie. I'm passing the puck. You call the shots now."

Carlie wondered what Leo had said to convince Damien to see her. It didn't matter. He was here now. She thought about taking his hand, hesitated, and kept her own in her lap.

"Well," she said, "I think we should get married, as soon as possible. Because I love you, and I'm tired of waiting, damn it. I want to test this out. I want to be allowed to experience all of it. No more stopping me." She chuckled, looking at the wall behind Damien, as if she could see through it. Damien's heart sped up. He looked at Carlie's collarbones, the soft skin of her neck. He finally touched her, tracing the contour of her cheek bone, starting at her scar, all the way to her chin, with the backs of his fingers.

"This weekend," he said.

"Can we really?"

"I'll arrange it. You don't worry about a thing. Draw. And eat. And sleep."

"Suits me!"

Hazel helped make the phone calls to book a slot at the town hall. She invited the families by phone—there was no time for mailing fancy little cards with embossed silver lettering. But the effect would have been the same. Carlie's parents didn't even know she was dating Damien, who they'd known for a very long time, though not well. They just dropped their heads.

"A second husband at twenty-five," Denise said.

"The first one died, honey. It doesn't really count," was Derek's reply.

Not organising the wedding was fabulous. Carlie had never been the kind of girl to dream of the perfect wedding, the perfect dress. She dreamed of skydiving, and freight-hopping. She had had a civil ceremony with Johnny as well, also last minute, with only a few friends as witnesses. While others paid thousands of dollars to wear a Cinderella dress once in their life, she had worn a black, knee-length skirt, a white satin, spaghetti-strap top, and ballet flats, all for under a hundred dollars. Total bargain. Johnny wore all black with a white tie. Their honeymoon was one date— they had a picnic dinner by the sea, spent hours drinking and spotting constellations, and stayed a night at a friend's vacant beach home. And that was enough for Carlie.

She made sure Damien understood how little she needed.

"I know," he had said, kissing her forehead. "You're the most laid-back girl I've ever known."

The time she didn't use working on her graphic novel she spent either with Hazel and Leo, taking walks, or indulging in her new practice. Tuesday morning, she had made her way to a small, rickety used-book store a few streets down. Read It Again, it was called. As per the clerk's suggestion, she had purchased the *Tao Te Ching*, teachings by Confucius, poetry by the mystic Rumí, the *Bhagavad Gita*, and a work called *The Seven Valleys*. Having contemplated a passage from one of the books, she would close her eyes and, still sitting with the words and what she could glean of their meaning, tune into the force she felt within her, and around her, beyond where her mind could imagine, beyond time and space. By the end of the week, she was able to control how quickly her threads spread out, but the experience was always expansive, full of light, and downright euphoric. Carlie wondered if it would always be this good.

Saturday came around too quickly. The morning air was electric, charged with the excitement that came with something as life changing as marriage. This also meant Damien and she would finally hit the sack. Do the deed. *Make the love.* She laughed, nervously pacing her apartment, wondering if she would get carried away and die, or if she would be able to keep her focus. How boring, she thought. In all the love songs and love stories written over the ages, Carlie was sure that none of them had made controlling their passion the focus, except maybe for the undead. She spent most of the early hours chasing images of bloodthirsty, fornicating vampires out of her head, shaking her fear-frozen fingers every so often to get her blood flowing. She couldn't imagine how pure, unspoiled newlyweds must feel on their wedding day. To know that something so big, so special, so anticipated was a sure thing, marked in the calendar months in advance . . . On the twenty-fifth of August, we have Julie here, and George, scheduled to *do it* for the first time. Cancel all other plans, people. This is happening. If she were Julie, she'd be crapping herself all day.

Well, she didn't, thank goodness. She didn't have much in the way of nails left, though. Still, the hour came and she showed up, sure of herself. This was happening.

A dozen people sat in the benches behind Carlie and Damien. The ceremony was simple. Perfectly so. Although it was a civil wedding and not a religious one, they read spiritual quotes that revolved around the idea that something greater than them was playing some interesting tricks and guiding them in marvellous ways. Carlie read a poem of her own:

Beloved of mine
Of below and above
A seed has grown
In the shade, in the sun
Towers now in my life, with blossoms and fruit
Sweetness, there is no sweeter than you
Of all the beauties
Inspiring my soul to its knees
Of all the melodies
That have bewitched me to dance
None have charmed me, none like you have
You are my divine Love
You are my eternal Romance.

Rings were exchanged. Hesitating to kiss, they kept it to a small peck. Boos rang loudly, as could be expected. So, Carlie straightened her lace dress, and, breathing in, clutched Damien's shoulders. She propped herself up on her tippy toes, he bent down. Her focus narrowed on his lips alone, she tried to not be distracted by her new husband's warm hands on her waist, or by how handsome he looked with his clean, trimmed beard, his suit and tie, or, hell, just by how much she loved him. They gave the crowd a kiss to holler about and pulled away quickly. Carlie's heart tickled with threads that felt tangled within her, fighting to come out but held in place by the strength of her will. Slightly dizzy, she held onto Damien.

"I got you," he whispered.

They turned to face their smiling family and friends.

17 Fairyland

Upon being saved from the decrepit fortress, OctoBitch clung to the WrenchKing's neck, so thrilled she was to have her love back. He picked her up in his arms and led her to his lair.

"You will live here now, with me. Safe," said the WrenchKing with authority.

"I'd live in an abandoned cave, shipwrecked on a desert island, or at the far ends of the galaxy on an inhospitable planet, struggling to live, if it meant being with you," OctoBitch said. She stood tall, for she was a proud shero, but inside she felt like the little girl she had been years ago, before heart-tentacle superpowers, before heartbreak, and before villains.

The WrenchKing's lair was relatively tidy, apart from the chemistry books, weaponry, and DIY how-to guides stacked on every surface. A fixing station for his various bio-mechanical body parts sat against a wall lined with wrenches of various sizes, hanging on hooks like trophies. A large double door in the back wall concealed what she guessed was the WrenchKing's sleeping quarters.

"How come you've never brought me here, Wrenchikins? What a dark, cosy place." She walked through the main area. "Quite the reader, you are. You must know how to make so many different kinds of wrenches." She ran her fingers over the titles in the stacks.

"I do." He put down his giant wrenches by the door. "I read about wrenches when I can't sleep. Then I dream about using them. Against *really bad* villains."

"Do you win?"

"Always," he said in his big-bodied voice.

An industrial-sized fridge towered in the corner of the eating area, where a large, stainless-steel table hugged the wall, a few chairs tucked under it. The WrenchKing opened the fridge to reveal a collection of large vials, filled with blue and green liquids. He took one out and poured it into a glass.

"What is this stuff?" OctoBitch asked.

"It's regenerative plasma tonic. You'll like it. But don't drink any of the green ones. They are the transmuting electric brew. I remember you not wanting to try that one again, Octi."

OctoBitch hadn't heard him say her name like that in a long time. Her heart nearly imploded on the spot. She sure loved that greasy WrenchKing.

"Oh, and don't drink the black ones in the back. They're for Master SpokeHand. He comes and plays cards on Tuesdays. I haven't told him, but it weakens his senses. So I always win. He owes me mountains and mountains of gold!" The WrenchKing howled with laughter.

"Oh, Wrenchikins." Octi wrapped her fingers around her glass of plasma tonic. "You can be so silly. One day Master SpokeHand will find out you've been cheating and you will be in big trouble."

The WrenchKing walked over to the steel table, where she had pulled out a chair, and lifted her up with his gigantic arms, sitting her on the table. She dropped her glass, which shattered on the ground, the blue plasma tonic spilling everywhere. But they didn't care. The WrenchKing had fought hard to be by his love's side, and when he had thought leaving was for the best, it destroyed them both. Defeating the PlushMen had not been easy, outnumbered four hundred to one, but he had triumphed and rescued his lady. And he was going to love her, forever, and right now, right there, on the metal table, if it was the last thing he ever did.

The WrenchKing kissed OctoBitch fiercely. Lo and behold, creeping, slithering, black, hungry tentacles came back to life, resuscitated by the WrenchKing's love. Or was it the regenerative plasma tonic? Her tentacles reached around his waist and crawled up to his throat. He ignored them. He had left her once because she almost killed him. She would certainly have learnt her lesson and be more careful now. Besides, OctoBitch and The WrenchKing could no longer resist their superhuman desire, and finally merged their bodies, throwing caution to the wind. They rocked like a tempestuous ocean; howling gales, roaring thunder, tidal waves and all. OctoBitch, in a frenzy of exhilaration, pierced the WrenchKing's torso with her tentacles, killing him on the spot.

Horrified at what she had done, she cried over his wounds, growls escaping between sobs. His russet blood covered the floor, swirling with her ink-black tears, until finally all became still. On her knees, wretched from so much weeping, she saw her reflection in the pool. And what a despicable thing she was. An inner hatred grew, filling her with a strange, new strength. She planted her foot in the pond of blood, splashing her lover's face as she stood. Her tentacles drove out of her at twice the size they ever had, ready to destroy whatever they could grab—villains, philanthropists, lovers. They would all taste the wrath of the revived OctoBitch.

The scenery of the countryside on the road to Alma was replaced with the characters Carlie had created, in a world where her superpowers were a danger to others instead of herself. She giggled from the passenger seat.

"What's funny?" Damien asked, driving.

"I think I figured out an ending to my graphic novel," she said. "It will call for a sequel."

"Really? That's great. So it's a happy ending?"

"Not really. Octobitch pulls a preying-mantis sort of move. I'm sorry, but you don't make it, Damien."

Chuckles filled the car, dying down in an unnatural way. They were silent the rest of the ride, clearly preoccupied. The possibility of Carlie being harmed made Damien question everything they were doing. He didn't think that their love, or her love for anyone else that could trigger her threads, was worth risking her life for.

They drove off the highway onto a gravel road which led them into the woods. The winding road curved tightly up a hill, the trees letting through only sporadic dashes of light, like lasers shot from the sky. They turned down a lane, tire tracks the only proof of civilisation. Grass grew high all around, wild flowers higher still. The lane opened up to a small, sun-drenched lot enclosed by an infantry of trees guarding a little wooden cabin with a gable roof. Damien parked the car on a pebbled strip in the freshly mowed front yard.

"Wait here," he told Carlie, stepping out. He walked around to her side to open her door.

"Ooh," Carlie said. "Thank you." She let him lead her by the hand into the fragrant outdoors and up the cabin's front steps. Once again he opened the door for her, and she stepped inside.

A beautiful afternoon light flooded the small living area, accentuating the golden colours of the wooden floors and walls. A cast-iron wood stove stood in a corner and, facing it, a vintage orange-and-brown-patterned couch and matching armchair. Homey. Damien ran back to get their bags while Carlie snooped, opening the cupboards, and then the fridge. They could survive at least a week without having to go anywhere.

"Hungry?" Damien asked, walking past with the bags and disappearing down the one hallway.

"No, just looking."

Damien reappeared with empty hands. He reached for hers. "Are you okay?"

"Ya. Should I not be?"

"No, of course. I mean, I'm just a bit worried. And nervous, I guess."

Carlie grinned and changed the subject, pointing to the space with a sweep of her eyes.

"This place is the sweetest, Damien. Is it yours?"

"Ya. Pa built it."

"What? That's crazy. He must have been such an amazing dad. You learned a lot from him?"

Damien frowned at the house in thought. "A fair amount. He was a hard worker. He didn't have much choice, what with being alone to care for me." He looked back at Carlie, now with a twinkle in his eye. "You wanna go for a walk? I wanna show you something."

Carlie followed him outside and around the back. An archway made with woven willow branches curved over an opening in the wall of trees lining the backyard.

"Fairyland," Carlie said.

"Um, maybe deer, and bears."

They walked no longer than a minute down the trail and then squeezed between some skinny, slanted timbers, seeming to have fallen perfectly into a natural barricade for the little child's fort built behind it. A space the size of a small bedroom had been cleared of trees, with only three tree stumps placed to the side as furniture. The rest was open and carpeted with grass and baby firs. A narrow, waist-high shelf, also crafted from woven willow, was attached to one of the walls.

"Damien," was all she said. Such magic could be felt here; an imaginary world, a secret place where a child could be anything, do anything.

"Kitchen." He pointed to the stumps, and then the open area. "Bed." Every fort needed a bed.

"Looks comfy," she said.

"I loved it here. It became a refuge for me after my mom died. Spent that first summer out here, every day, all day. Pa would even let me spend the night, with blankets and a pillow on a camping mat. I used to stare at the stars until I feel asleep, thinking she might be up there, watching. Then Pa explained that the skies are full of suns, planets, and flying rocks. That it was beautiful, but no place for an angel. He said her soul was somewhere we couldn't see with our eyes, or feel with our hands, but that she was close, close enough to hear my prayers and give me good night kisses. Good ol' Pa-Fern."

They stepped out, the magic of the fort accompanying them as they walked back through the woods to the cabin. Damien led the way, clearly in his element, and Carlie watched him, wondering how many stories and surprises he had stashed away, happy to have a lifetime to discover them all.

Inside, Damien started a fire in the wood stove and they prepared some food together. Nervous looks were exchanged. They slowed down when their bodies brushed against each other, paused when their hands touched. The food was simple and delicious, but Carlie's stomach was so knotted she could hardly eat. Their conversation was limited to small strings of words between long silences, commenting on the meal, the smell of the burning wood, the sky as the sun set behind the trees in the front yard.

"This is perfect, Damien. I'm so happy. I'm sorry if I'm not more verbal about it."

"It's all good. I thought you might like it here," he said from over his empty plate, taking a sip of water. He cleared his throat, pushed back his chair and stood up. Carlie watched him come to her.

"My wife." He smiled, holding out his hand. She took it, interlacing her fingers with his. They walked through the little hallway and into the warm glow of the back room. It was one large bedroom, taking the width of the whole cabin. On the back wall, three large, square windows faced the woods, the headboard of a large bed with a thick grey-and-red plaid comforter pushed up against the middle one. A chandelier hung from the diagonally rising ceiling beam, creating gleams of dancing lights over the wooden floor and walls. They stood on the edge of a red, circular shaggy carpet.

"Fairyland," Carlie said again.

"Um, maybe goblins, and more bears." Damien stroked his beard with a sly grin.

Carlie walked around. There weren't many objects on the furniture. There was a jewellery box, which she opened. A ballerina spun magnetically to a haunting, pluckity tune. Carlie lifted the little dancer. The music stopped, and started again as she placed her back down. Beside it were some candles, and a dark-green peace lily, with one white, almond-shaped flower blooming unpretentiously. She turned around. Damien stood in the middle of the room at the centre of the red carpet, staring at her.

"You look worried," she said, laughing a little. She knew he was waiting for her. She was the one with the plan.

"I *am* worried," he said. "But I think I want to hold you in my arms now."

Carlie smiled, the nervous knot shooting up her torso, settling in her head gently, giving her a slight buzz. She joined him. "Um, it might be less romantic than you're used to, but I hope you will humour me."

"That's the plan." He breathed in deeply to calm his anticipation.

"Sit," she said.

"Here?"

"Yes, please. On the floor."

Damien sat where he had been standing. Carlie went to her bag and came back with a book. Damien frowned.

"A how-to?"

"You wish!" She sat in front of him, their knees touching. "Look, I've been meditating on this stuff, and I'm gaining a bit of familiarity with my energy because of it."

"Energy?"

"My nirvana threads, you know? Anyway, I love this stuff. It's beautiful, it's moving . . . It triggers the deepest, most divine part of me, and it makes me think, too. Every time I read, I understand more about life, about existence, about myself."

She paused, looking for the right words.

"I think being close to you was weakening me because there was no way my heart could sustain it. Like I was short-circuited. It was too powerful."

Damien grinned and nodded, taking it as a compliment.

"Silly boy," Carlie said. "This here is like a way for me to re-wire myself. Behind the veil of what we see, whatever is out there is feeding me an endless amount of the most delicious energy. If this works . . ." She looked at him, her mouth watering. "It's going to be good."

18 Hurts So Good

"And if it doesn't?" Damien asked.

"Then, I die?"

"I have a first aid kit."

"That's not going to help, I'm afraid."

Damien nodded, thinking. "We don't have to do this, Carlie."

"Damien, I can't even hold your hand without my lights seeking you out. I'm not going to let this freak phenomenon rob me of a life with you, however abnormal it turns out to be. I love you."

Damien nodded again, forcing a smile.

Carlie opened the book to a dog-eared page. She closed her eyes and breathed, clearing her head before opening them again to read. Damien did the same, but kept his shut, listening to the words intoned. They were beautiful, hinting at the majesty and mystery of life's inner reality. This was new to him; he had never meditated, or prayed, with anyone before. It was a different kind of intimacy. One where souls, not just bodies, got closer.

It wasn't long before Carlie began feeling herself expand. She knew what was coming, and allowed it to happen without resisting. Lights wriggled out of her chest, her arms, her legs, her head—glowing rivulets travelling to and from her as she became filled to overflowing with that glorious love she was now getting used to. She looked up. Damien was watching her, the quick rise and fall of his chest the only movement behind his own hovering threads. His eyes were a blend of curiosity, concern, and desire.

"Your turn," she said.

Damien stretched his arm out to caress Carlie's hair, lingering at her cheek to pass his thumb over her lower lip. A different feeling climbed into Carlie's circuitry, but she was glad to see the throbbing expansiveness didn't wane. A few of her threads poked out towards him like bifurcating veins of electricity, and, connecting with his, sent jolts of pleasure through her body.

Damien inched himself nearer, uncrossing his legs, careful that his movements didn't disturb what he thought was a delicate situation.

"You're so beautiful, my wife." His lips brushed over her temple and down her cheek. Kissed the corner of her mouth. Carlie's heart rate accelerated until she felt it thumping in her limbs. Struggling to keep her mind on the energy coursing through her, she watched many more finger-like threads crawl around Damien's torso, over his shoulders, enveloping him.

"Holy shit," she whispered.

Damien pulled his head back to look into her eyes.

"Don't stop," she said, reaching behind his back and pulling him closer. So he didn't. His mouth pressed against her waiting lips, their tongues crashing in between. A small whimper escaped her, her eyes closing and opening like butterfly wings as they kissed. Pressure rising from the top of her head, she reached her arms around him and wrapped him with body and light.

Then she stopped cold.

Damien couldn't see what Carlie was experiencing in terms of heart threads, and the *Source*, as they had previously called it, and had no idea what her mind-state was. He could tell that she was more contained than during the other few heated moments they had shared, and he wasn't sure how good of a thing that was. Because at that moment, she was as still as a statue. Though he hungered for her more than ever, he followed her lead and waited.

With a slight frown, Carlie grasped the bottom of Damien's shirt and pulled it off. Relief and excitement rushed through him. A mischievous smile at his lips, he reached for the hem of her lace dress. She lifted herself off the ground just enough for him to pull it up and over her. For a moment he just stared, not expecting her to have nothing on underneath. She gave him a nod, smiling but serious. Cautious. He moved in and placed his lips on her neck, pulling her close against him. The rest of his clothing was peeled off as Carlie became more secure, more grounded. Her lights branched out explosively, its current moving freely through both their bodies, their lips, the tips of their fingers, increasing the more ignited they became. Her spirit was so full, Damien could never take that away, no matter how much love she gave him. All worries dissipated, her resistance vanished, and she let herself get as hot and carried away as she had been dreaming, and this time Damien let her. They rocked like a tempestuous ocean; howling gales, roaring thunder, tidal waves and all.

The sun beamed in from the east-facing windows and lit the room afire. Carlie looked over at her sleeping lover before slipping her legs over the edge of the bed. A pair of arms appeared at her sides and tightened around her waist, pulling her back in. Damien kissed the back of her ear and the side of her neck. It was great to not worry about falling sick from love. Full of gratitude, she turned to kiss him, threads jumping out, forwards and upwards simultaneously, sending a rush of beautiful emotion through her: a blend of physical desire and spiritual love, both for him and for Life. She didn't know if she'd ever be able to kiss him again without being so fulfilled. That was fine by her.

"You marvellous creature," Damien said, exploring the silkiness of her nightshirt. Warm, honey love, and it was hours before they came down from their ecstasy, and finally out of bed.

She pulled out her pill bottles from her bag and went to the kitchen to make breakfast. Crêpes, fruit, coffee. Simplicity. Now that the complications had made way for ease, she felt, as if for the first time, thankful for her strange heart. For the life she was permitted to have. For the poem, brought to her by the wind.

After another dreamy day and night of food, magical woods and passion at the Moore cabin, they drove back to Mootpoint in Damien's 1963 baby-blue Pontiac Catalina Hardtop Coupe. "Blue car" was no longer acceptable, apparently.

Carlie moved into his lair upon their return. His fridge was full of normal human food, and on his walls hung posters of bands, not wrenches. He would not be dying from her piercing lust, and, gladly, neither would she. But the WrenchKing did, and when Carlie brought her drawings to Matt at the Brick Tower Publishing House, they took it as is, and signed her for another two. An OctoBitch trilogy.

And it was all great.

Yet, something was missing. She kept up her practice, meditating and finding new sources of wisdom to draw from. Not only because it insured that she could have the romantic life she wanted with Damien, but because it fed her. All of her. There was no trade-off, no unwanted side-effects. The nirvana threads thrived, growing in strength, beauty and emotion. Sometimes she thought it couldn't keep getting better. And it did. But still, there was a hole.

She had the book deal and a fabulous relationship with her brother. Hazel's baby was on the way. Carlie didn't want to be a mother just yet. That wasn't what she longed for. She managed to have dinner every few weeks with her parents while they were in town, but they were gone more often than not. But that didn't bother her either.

"What's wrong then?" asked Damien, leaning over to look at Carlie who was lying on the floor, staring at the ceiling.

"I don't know."

"How was your last appointment?"

"Everything is tippity top. Their minds are officially *blown*."

"Well, I sure am happy for that. You don't seem so happy, though. Carlie, are you not happy?"

She sat up and faced him, scratching the top of her head as she searched for the right words.

"I'm alive, Damien."

"Yes, you sure are." He held back a laugh.

"But I wasn't meant to be."

Damien saw her meandering in her inner world, baiting her guilt to the surface.

"I don't want to tell you how to feel," Damien said. "I haven't been through the things you have. But I for one am deeply thankful to that person who gave you a heart. And even to that person who missed out on his or her chance to get it. You're here thanks to them."

"That's kind of the problem," Carlie said. Damien shook his head, not getting it. "My life is not worth more than theirs, or anyone else's. Even if I am happy. It's because I *am* happy now that I feel this crappiness inside. I was too busy before. Too busy grieving, and trying to just freaking survive, understanding how to cope with my crazy, magical heart. Now, things are in order, I mean—I'm not dying, I've found love . . ." She cracked a grin. "I even have a dream job I never even considered dreaming about. I have this beautiful life to enjoy, and I feel so guilty about it."

Carlie's heart tightened in her chest. She clenched her fists as tears poured down her cheeks.

"Whoa there." Damien hurried to her side, down on the floor. His arms around her, Carlie buried her face in his neck and bawled.

"I'm so happy," she said as she gasped for air between sobs. Damien caressed her back, trying to figure out how to make sense of what she was going through.

"Once, you told me you could write an anonymous letter to the donor's family. Maybe it's time to thank them."

The crying subsided to snivels.

"See, I should've thought of that myself. Just proves how selfish I am."

"If you were that selfish, you wouldn't be having this breakdown right now. You feel guilty about your joy, Carlie. Thats's not usually the kind of thing selfish people feel guilty about."

"My joy could have been someone else's."

"Ya, but it's not. Life gave it to you."

Carlie didn't speak or move for a few minutes, caged in Damien's arms. He finally released her and got up.

"I'll make you tea."

Johnny stood in the middle of the kitchen as Carlie paced before him, whining on and on about the rent, the bills, his expensive smoking habit. They were short that month, just as they were every month, but this time the landlord wasn't giving them any leeway. They would be out on the street come the next day if they didn't get their hands on some money. Johnny just stood there, saying nothing. Carlie eventually slinked down to the floor and cried.

"Maybe," Johnny finally said, "you could ask your parents for a handout."

She shook her head. They already didn't like Johnny. They would just blame him for not pulling his weight, and she wouldn't let that happen. She preferred owning up to her shit.

That day, a random cheque came in the mail. A tax return adjustment. It covered the rent, to the penny. Carlie and Johnny couldn't help but believe in life's benevolence after that. They just needed to have faith. And keep working. And maybe quit smoking.

19 Open Door

Carlie sat at the table in front of a piece of lined paper, a pen neatly placed along its edge. Too hot to drink, her green tea waited on her left, the steam rising in curls, its smell enough to calm her nerves. She wiped a few pearls of tears lingering in her lower lashes. Damien placed his hand on her right shoulder and pecked her on her left cheek. She turned, making sure she got a proper kiss before he left for the shop. The usual bliss reverberated through her bones.

"Mmm, that's better," Damien said, seeing a smile settle on Carlie's face.

She turned to her paper as he dissolved into the light pouring in through the open door. He left it open.

Dear family, she wrote.

I am the person who received your loved one's heart. I am finally writing today to express my gratitude. I know what it's like to lose someone you love. I lost my husband in the car crash that almost took my life. Grief is a hauntingly difficult thing to live with. I am sincerely sorry for your loss.

I wanted to let you know that, though I am nobody special and no more deserving than anyone else at a second chance at life, I am truly happy today that I received such a gift. I've married again. I'm working doing something that I love, and I try to be a good, caring person on a day-to-day basis.

Though I doubt I will always succeed at leading the most praiseworthy life, I wanted to let you know that I will honour this wonderful, magical heart by always doing my best. I am truly, incredibly thankful.

Carlie put the pen down. She felt the dark presence that had been creeping up on her slink away through the door of light. Octobitch was going to perdure on paper only.

The real Carlie was going to find a way to give back.

Thanks

Mike Parr, for sharing so generously your experience with your heart transplant, blowing my mind with beautiful, interesting details one wouldn't expect could happen in such a situation. Surely you are a special soul. Lynne Vokes-Leduc for connecting me with Mike. I would have never found him without you. Thank you! Doctor and friend Ruth Vander Stelt, for sharing your knowledge in emails and over the phone, squeezing me in your busy schedule. You gave me hard info, and with it I was able to make my story even more magical. Funny how that worked out! You are a gem. Sherwin Sullivan Tija, for taking the time to show me your process for creating graphic novels and answering all my questions, and Nathan Wilkinson, for connecting me with Sherwin, and for calming my nerves, Skyping with me from across the oceans when I was overwhelmed with the decision to make the accompanying graphic novel in the first place. You're a real friend. My family, of course, for their support and endless enthusiasm, and my parents, for raising me in a way where my spirituality was nurtured, as well as my (punk-ass) individuality. Lastly, a thanks to all the mystical poems the wind brings through my life in the form of words, music, art, and friends.

Please enjoy Carlie Jones' *OctoB*tch and the WrenchKing*.

Carlie Jones'

OctoB*tch
AND THE
Wrenchkng

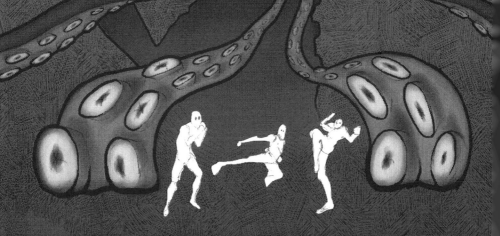

art & story by Rachel Tremblay

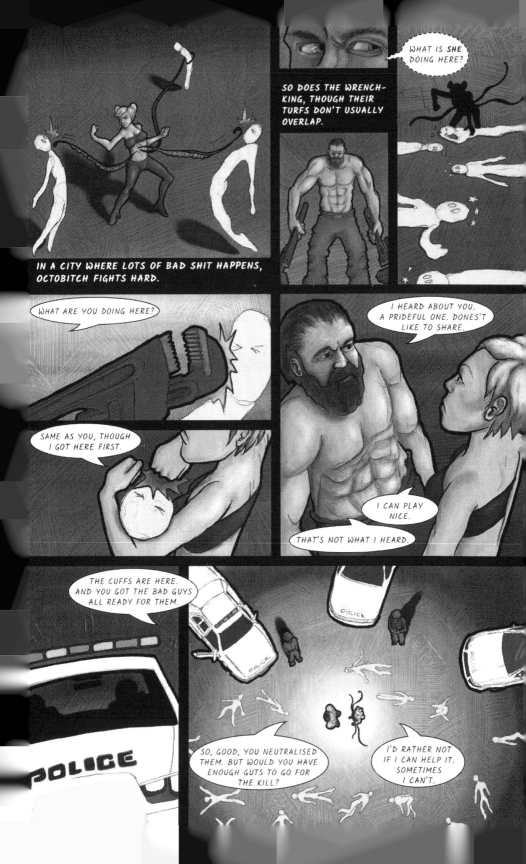

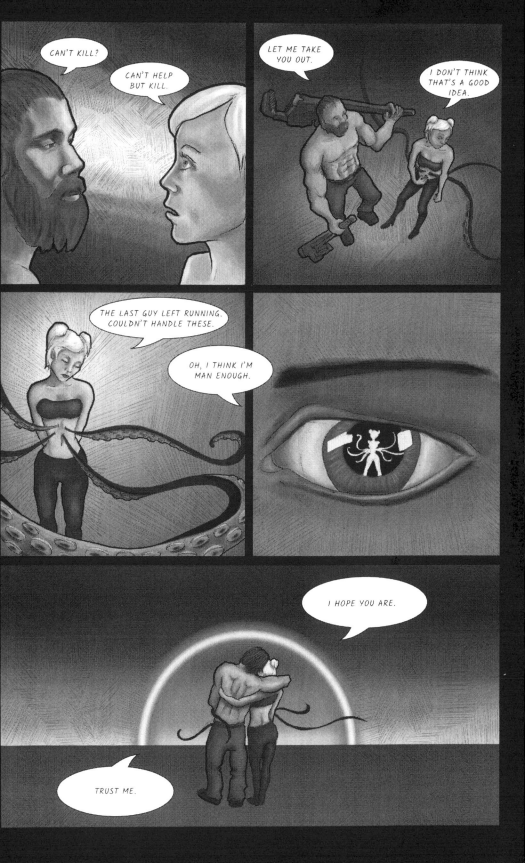

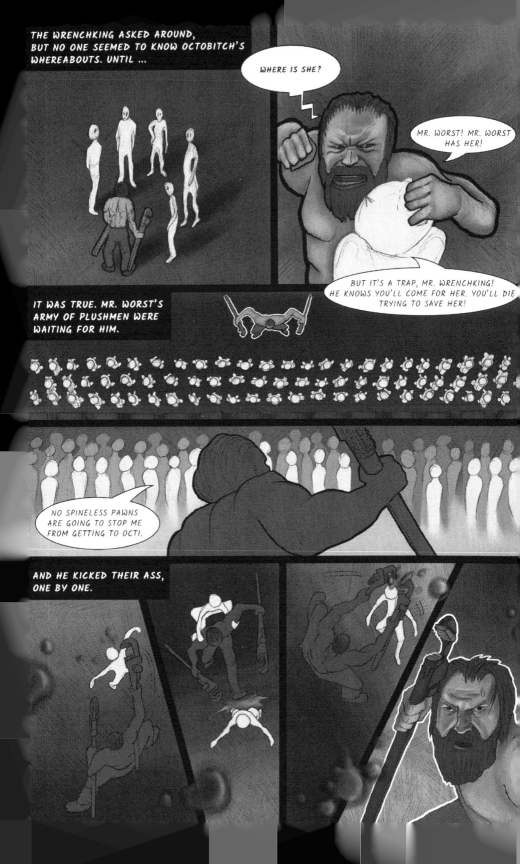

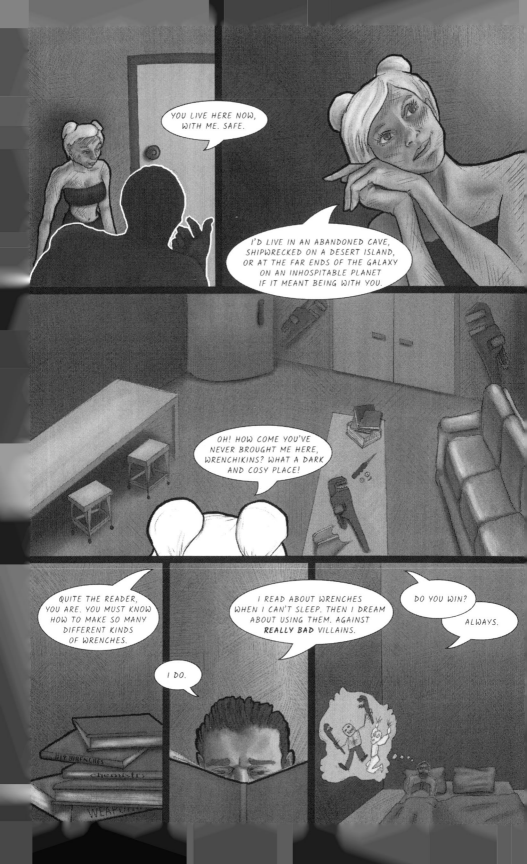

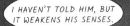

Rachel Tremblay is a Canadian writer, poet, visual artist, and musician. In no particular order, her time on earth has up to yet been a medley of recording music albums, gigging, writing rhymes, phat markers, skateboarding, raving, yoga, espresso slinging, going to shows, capoeira, graphic design, tattoos, travelling, community service, drawing, painting, marrying, making babies, and homeschooling. Author to the high fantasy novel "Topaz: The Truth Portal & The Color Mayhem", she digs all things that can be twisted like magical play dough.

www.rachel-tremblay.com

27476280R00096

Made in the USA
Lexington, KY
04 January 2019